COMPLICATIONS OF A TROUBLED HEART

Diamond Key

ISBN-13: 978-1-964234-24-3

PAPERBACK

THANK YOU

I would like to thank Lee's Press and Publishing Company for formatting my book, and Cara and her team for being patient with me on this journey. Lorenzo for giving me that inspiring thought to write a book. And to some friends at my work who read it and gave me some feedback as well—Shelby Lee, Annette, Fancy Fancy, and Kelly just to name a few. And to my idol, Z, who gave me the support to push on whenever it got tough and to believe in the process and myself.

DEDICATION

This book is dedicated to my mom. She was my biggest supporter, but I lost her in September 2023. My world was rocked. I decided it was time to make my dream a reality. You always told me I could do whatever or become whatever as long as I put my mind to it. My guardian angel, Pamela Hall. I completed this book so feel free to read it in Heaven. Love you always, Mommy, and thank you for giving me the courage to make my dream of becoming an author a reality.

INTRODUCTION

This is about a black woman working to become the best lawyer and make a name for herself. However, she is stressed. She decides to go on a trip and meets a Spanish man, who she falls in love with. Years later they get married, and she starts to find out things about her husband's past. In addition, she finds herself having a brief affair with her boss on a trip. But as she tries to keep her happy family together, she is still deeply in love with her husband, but she also has feelings for her boss. Torn between finding out her husband's past and having feelings for her boss she doesn't want to admit to, she is also faced with having information about a close friend's death. Only to find her husband's name involved in the case. Her will is tested and, she will do anything to make sure her happy family stays happy, even lie to protect the ones she loves, even if her husband is suspect number one.

My name is Na'keya Marie Williams. How would I describe myself? Well, I'm just your average, curvy, southern born type gal who dreams about finding herself a prince charming. He will take her to his castle and give her that happily ever after. In reality, there is no happy ending.

I'm currently working at a job that I can't stand. I'm going back to school full-time to become a lawyer. I should finish school in three years if all goes well. I'm making pretty good money. But when I first started, it was very difficult because of the circumstances that I was facing at that time. I had to move and relocate to another city while still in school. I had to find another school, send for my previous transcripts, and it was just difficult to be uprooted from my support system and move to a completely different town where I knew no one.

I used to work at the law office of Kirk and Kirk, a family-owned business. I worked there for nearly two in a half year. One day, out of the blue, they started laying people off. Guess who was one of them. That's when I decided to change my ways in life. I had to move and downsize to accommodate my style.

I started at Gable & Andersons, where I met my sister from another mister Allison. She is not your average 28-year-old Italian girl. She's a mix of your curvy, hip hop talking-type chic, with a touch of soul. She loves skydiving and surfing, and she always speaks her mind. Only thing is she is very hush hush when it comes to talking about the love department. Always looking for Mr. Right Now, but always seems to run away from Mr. Future Husband. Happiness is right in front of you. She always says she's not ready to be wifey but likes to practice the wifey duties. We never see eye to eye on marriage. We would argue for hours about the single life versus the married life. But no matter, she's my girl and we just have to realize our views about marriage are very different.

4

One day, Alli called me up, just like every morning, but this morning was different. Usually, I would be at work around nine, but due to taking a mini vacation to vent from an exhausted week of a complicated case the week before, I was home resting to clear my mind for the next case. She says, "Hey, let's take a trip all out of the blue."

"I can't replied Nakeya."

"And why not asked Allison?"

"I have some work to do Nakeya says. You don't says Allison."

"This is the perfect time to take a trip and clear your head. Make a fresh start on next week. Come on, you only live once."

I tried to think of every excuse in the book. She was begging and pleading with me. Next thing I knew, we were at the airport heading to Argentina.

When we first arrived there, I thought, Alli...what have I let you talk me into?

"It's so beautiful here."

"I know right, girl. Let's go get checked in."

We unpacked our suitcases and changed into our beach clothes, leaving the room and heading towards the beach. We enjoyed our Mai Tais by the beach, and talked about how white the sand was. I glanced over and that's when I laid eyes on the most gorgeous man, my husband-to-be and soulmate, Rafael Juan Romas.

"Allison you see what I see?"

"Where oh yeah the sexiest guy I have ever seen."

He was getting out of the water, and my heartbeat was so fast. He was tall, athletically built with a muscular chest, slightly broad shoulders, a body like a god for a Latino man. While he swam toward the shore, all I could do was stare and imagine those arms around me, laying on that chest and his eyes; green like emeralds. I have never seen a Latino with green eyes. I was mesmerized. He had long curly hair neatly pulled back into a ponytail and wore a blue pair of speedos, definitely filling it out in all the right spots, if you know what I mean.

I was thinking inappropriate thoughts so maybe that is why when he first said hola, I said nothing. I looked as if I saw a ghost or something. Hey, Earth to Na'keya, say something, I told myself.

"Sorry, you say something Nakeya says smiling to herself?

"Sí [yes] . Welcome, my name is Rafael Juan Romas, your tour guide."

As it got later into the evening, we headed back to the room, showered, and changed. Later on that night we met up with Rafael. He had on a nice blue shirt with khaki shorts and sandals. Allison wore a nice semi long yellow strapless dress with matching sandals. She pinned some of her hair up with long ringlets hanging on her shoulder. I wore my strapless pink dress with ruffles and matching pink loafers, deciding to wear my hair down since it was up earlier.

We went to this club Rafael suggested. We ordered some drinks and sat down at a booth.

"Would you like to dance?"

"I would love to. You have a lovely accent."

"Thank you."

He smells so good! We started dancing fast, then the music slowed down, and he placed my body next to his. I laid my head on his athletic chest to get a closer sniff of his cologne or soap. Whatever it was smelt so good.

6

Your husband is lucky and a fool to leave such a beautiful woman like you alone."

"Huh? Oh no, I am not married, nor do I have a man." Why did I say that? I don't know where that came from. He held me tighter after I said that.

"I liked that club a lot."

"Perhaps we shall do it again."

"I would like that. Thanks for walking us back to the villa."

"See you ladies mañana [tomorrow]."

"Sweet dreams...bye"

"Adiós señoras [bye ladies] ."

The very next morning we met Rafael for breakfast.

"Buenos días, señoras [Good morning ladies] ."

"Morning Rafael they replied."

Allison seemed to catch on to us vibing because, out of nowhere, she made up an excuse to go back to the room.

"May I show you around Nakeya?"

All I could do was smile. As the week went on me and Rafael got really close. He started telling me his dreams about how he wanted to travel back to the states and someday own his own business.

"You should come back to the states and maybe you could someday run your own business. Anything is possible."

We talked about our dreams for hours it seemed. That's when he leaned over and kissed me. "Wow, incredible. I'm sorry, you're a very bonita [beautiful] woman."

I kissed him back. For our final night in Argentina, we all decided to go to the club.

"I'm gonna miss you when you leave"

"This doesn't have to be goodbye, you know."

We both leaned in towards each other to kiss. Later on that night, I met up with Rafael on the beach. We walked along the shore hand in hand. We kissed and talked more about our dreams, then we laid out on the blanket, looking up at the stars.

"Make a wish."

"What you wish for"? Before I could react, Rafael leaned over and began kissing me. I kissed him back. Then we began dancing to our own music inside our heads. When I looked in his eyes, I could see my unborn children. We looked back up at the stars again. He kissed my neck, and I began rubbing his back. He slowly started rubbing my breast, sucking my nipples gently. He made his way up my dress. All I could hear was the ocean in the background.

We're getting more into it and he slowly opened my legs.

"Are you sure you want to Nakeya asked Rafael?"

Before I knew it, he was thrusting in and out. I began moaning and tingling from ecstasy. As I began cumming he kissed my forehead, then said softly in my ear "I would follow you anywhere."

I just looked at him as I gathered my thoughts and tried to register in my head what just happened. We quickly got dressed and then he walked me back to my room.

"See you later, mi amor [my love] ."

As I crawled into my bed, Allison said, "You two have fun?"

"Oh, Alli...I had the most amazing time tonight."

Later on, that morning as I started packing to go back home, the door to the room opened. Allison, where have you been?

"You like Rafael Allison asked Nakeya?"

"Who Nakeya said then said yes, I think I could fall—" No not the love word Allison looked surprisingly . Maybe Allison says Nakeya not looking up.

"Hold on, chica [girl]".

"Let's go. You got everything Allison asked Nakeya?"

Yes, Nakeya replied, walking out the hotel room.

We made our way to the airport, but I kept looking back at the doors.

"Who are you looking for Allison?"

Nakeya turned and gasped at Rafael. Tears filled my eyes.

"I told you, I would follow you anywhere."

I looked at Allison. "You did this?"

"Yes. Y'all looked sad, and I wanted to make you two happy."

And five years later, we are still in love. When Rafael first came, he worked so hard. With the help of my dad's dear friends Lou Eger and his brother Charu, Rafael was able to start his own business building homes and concreting in no time. They helped give Rafael a kickstart in starting his very own business. They were like my uncles when I was growing up. So, when they offered to help Rafael, we were so pleased. Now Rafael's business is very successful and called Trinity's Casa [house] a dream come true.

I try to visit him every day just to see his smile. I bring him a vanilla chai and for lunch, carne asada with jalapeños. His company is downtown, fourteen blocks from my office. Whenever I go to the office, I can't keep my hands off him. I take an early lunch just so I *can make love to him. In his office, I lock the door behind us, and we make love. We start kissing; he is pulling up my skirt. I open my thighs, pulling him closer. I feel him go deeper and deeper. The closer to our climax we get, the faster he goes. To keep me from making noise, he puts his finger in my mouth to suck on.*

After a quick shower, it's back to our jobs. We go like nothing happened. We just moved into our new house. We used to live in an apartment in the city, but we decided we needed more room, so we found a house in the suburbs, not far from the city. A four bedroom, two in a half bath with a full finished basement. We use the basement whenever we entertain guests from his job or mine.

His parents, Roman and Rosetta, live with us. They moved in about a year after we did. His dad got really sick and had to leave his job. That was when Rafael told them to move with us to cut their expenses. At first, it was a difficult move for his parents. They were used to living on their own. As time passed, it got better for them. We learned to share a space and not want to kill one another. Mama Rosetta always cooks dishes from their native country. I love to see her in the kitchen, she seems right at home.

Rafael's sister Maria is married to Jose. Maria and Jose met each other in college and fell in love. I want to tell you about how Jose and Maria met. It was quite unexpected. Jose was in pre-med, and Maria was also, but then transferred out after three and a half months. Maria, one day, was studying for a test and Jose needed to be tutored. Well, they met and everything he said to her seemed to be the wrong thing. He got nervous when he saw her. Maria was talking to me, and I heard a guy in the background starting to sing. The room we were in was mine. Maria happened to be there. So, he began singing her favorite song. The more he sang the song, the more she seemed to smile and gave into his proposal. They went on a date that weekend and decided to go skiing. Only to get snowed into the ski lodge!

Maria missed her ride with me and got stuck there. Had she not gotten stuck there, they would not have fallen in love with each other. That night, as they were getting warm by the fireplace, Jose leaned over and gave her a gentle kiss.

"I can be romantic. You make me nervous, and I get tongue tied."

Just then Maria leaned over and kissed him back and began rubbing his back. Maria and Jose put down their cups of hot chocolate and started to undress each other in her room. The radio was playing a song that seemed to fit the mood. He took off her shirt that was wet from skiing, and she then took off his, before starting to feel his nice athletic chest. He worked his way down her body, and she arched her back from anticipation as he slowly kissed her navel and licked in between her inner thighs. She screamed for more. He just made her shake uncontrollably. That night, he stayed in her room, and they snuggled.

After three days, they began talking. After the Christmas holiday was over, Jose went back into his pre-med classes happier and smarter, thanks to Maria, and she started her pre-law classes. After dating for nearly three and a half years, Jose one day comes to the house with flowers and asks her dad for Maria's hand in marriage. At first her dad said no, and Jose didn't know he was playing a mean joke. He stormed out of the kitchen. But Jose, who was scared, started pledging his love for Maria to her daddy. Her dad played it off. Looking mean, he said, "If anyone can come to me and stand your ground like a grown man and pledge their love for my daughter, then I guess you're the guy for her."

"What Maria said, half crying half laughing?"

"Sorry, I couldn't keep my face straight any longer," her Dad said! You two have my blessings, he told them as he held Maria in his

arms.

"Oh, Daddy Maria cried!"

A couple of months later, Maria called me. I was still working at my old law firm at that time.

"Na'keya."

"Hey, girl. I want you to come to my wedding"

"Your?"

"Yes, gurl, I'm getting married!"

"Girl! When? We need to shop, and I want you to be my maid of honor."

"Of course, you'll be my maid of honor."

"I gotta get in shape."

"You look great."

"Okay, I will be there two days before."

"Love you!"

On the day of the wedding, I was getting my hair done. It was not how I wanted it, but I still rocked it. I wore a dark gold strapless prom gown. It accentuated my curves in all the right places. My shoes were black, semi-high because of my accident a few months before, I could not wear real high heels.

Jose and his groomsmen were all dressed in white tuxedos accented with the same color shirt as our dresses and black boots, but it was hard to tell. I remember seeing a guy there, but he stayed mostly hidden like he was in hiding. I think that was Rafael.

The reception was suddenly cut short due to Maria getting ill. We later found out she had a tubal pregnancy and miscarried. Two months later they got news she was pregnant with twins. We were at a carnival and Maria's phone rang.

"Hello. Yes, this is she." Maria had gone to the doctors for the flu and was waiting for the doctor's call. When Dr. Yen called and told her she was three weeks pregnant, Maria nearly fainted. Meanwhile, Jose fell out of the ride after hearing the news. About seven and a half months later, they welcomed two healthy twin boys. One named Adrian Mateo Gomas, weighing five pounds and two ounces, and Tomas Ronan Gomas, weighing five pounds and eight ounces. Born on the Fourth of July...and the rest of their story is history.

Jose became a doctor as he planned, and Maria became a lawyer. Maria became one of my many dearest and closest friends in college. Jose's older brother Juan is married to a woman named Lydia from New York, the big apple. They are expecting twin girls. Juan met Lydia while at a concert while staying in New York on a mini getaway. I remember it as if it was yesterday.

Juan had tickets to go to the Mark Anthony concert. He was running late and he almost missed the bus. He began making his way to his seat when he laid eyes on Lydia. She has a bottle shape, sexy mixed chic dress with curly dark brown hair. Her eyes are hazel and make you think of sleep. On his way down the steps, he bumped into her and made her lose her ticket. When the concert started, she couldn't find the ticket. He heard her arguing with the ticket man, who happened to be buddies with him since the first grade. He told Frank to let her in. She thanked him.

Then he says, "you have to sit here."

"Wow, are you serious? This is the box..."

"Yes, and you will have to have dinner with me afterwards."

"That sounds like a plan."

Well, after the concert, they went to the coffee house and got coffee and a pineapple pizza. They begin talking, and next thing you know; they're dating. Juan moved to New York, found a job and stayed there for one year. Within that year, they moved in with one another and Juan told Lydia to move with him back to his home state. Lydia was not so sure at first, but then Juan told her to take a chance and that she was his Ying to his yang. They moved back here, and Lydia got pregnant not long after. Juan proposed to Lydia, and they got married on his boss's yacht.

Lydia wore a tight-fitting mermaid style wedding gown. Juan wore a black tuxedo with a sky-blue shirt. Me, Maria, and her sister Chelsea were dressed in sky-blue dresses made differently with matching high heels. I don't remember Rafael there, I guess that was when he was living over in Argentina. That evening was a blur. As Lydia gathered the single ladies around, Allison pushed me forward.

"You should catch the bouquet."

"Who would I marry?

"We will find someone tall, dark, and don't forget, handsome."

"Yes, handsome."

I caught the bouquet!

"Don't say a word, Maria."

"Look, don't say anything either Allison!

"Let's dance," Willy Nakeya says, looking mad at Maria and Allison as they smiled."

"Okay."

Later on, that night, I dreamed of my future wedding. How all the people looked so happy for us. Then it shifted into our honeymoon. We were on an exotic island, and we were kissing. My mystery man moves down towards my neck, then he kisses each side of my breasts as he moves closer and closer to my pelvic region. I moan louder, and then as I get ready to reach for his head, the alarm rings!

Wow, that seemed more lifelike than the ones last week. I need to find a friend, Nakeya says to herself, but I always wonder why I can never see his face she asked herself while shaking her head?

I get up and get ready to go to work, and the rest of their story is history. Juan now owns a mechanic shop and Lydia goes to school for massage therapy and does hair at the salon on Third and Nine downtown. One thing I always notice with each wedding I attend; I often dream of the one I want to have someday. I can see it so clearly. Oh, how I hope my prince charming will come save me from my life. I daydream of how I would react and what we would do to keep our love for one another vibrant.

And then there is Enrique, the baby of the family. He's a landscaper at Rafael's place. Quite the playboy. Every Sunday, we have our famous Sunday dinners where we talk about family business, news, and what's going on in our lives at that time. Mama always teases Enrique, who is someone's new flavor of the month. How long will we see her? he always says. I have too much love to just share it with one girl.

My family lives far away, but I keep in touch with them on a regular basis. The reason why Enrique said he would never fall back in love if he could help it was because of one girl in the neighborhood; Marisel. They were high school sweethearts. Where you saw one, you saw the other. One day, Enrique goes to surprise her at her home only to find her in the arms of another man. Her other boyfriend.

Enrique asked her why she would hurt him. She replied, "I'm only doing what guys have been doing to women for years. I did love you as I was cumming, but after the urge left."

Enrique told her all he remembered was hearing the laughter between them. Going back home to deal with his sorrow, he vowed to never fall in love unless it was real. So, from that day on he would love 'em, then sex 'em; no call or just block them from his phone. That is why he's a player. Not giving his heart to anyone because his heart was broken so badly. He figures if you don't put your heart into someone, you can't get hurt. He was only worrying about himself being hurt, he didn't care if the girl got hurt.

My parents have been married for twenty-five years, and they come to visit on the holidays if they're not already traveling. My dad is retired, and always talks about the law, this law or that law. That is why I got into law. Mom was a registered nurse, she retired two years ago. How my mom and dad met was romantic. They lived near each other when they were small and used to walk to school together. My dad would share his crackers and cheese with my mom when they would play outside. As they got older in middle school, they rode the bus together. My dad would pull my mom's hair to impress his buddies, who at that age thought girls had cooties. But when he was alone with her in the backyard, he was a perfect gentleman.

Before they knew it, they were in high school, and he finally got up the nerve to ask my mom to go out with him. Prom was approaching and he asked my mom to go. He wore a light brown suit and black shoes his dad outgrew. My mom wore a chocolate brown dress, which showed her curves and some black heels. As my dad watched my mom come down the stairs, my grandfather would give him the evil eye, but he somehow knew that would be his future son-in-law.

My dad saw my mom come down behind my grandma and said she was the most beautifulest girl he had ever laid eyes on. He noticed that night how grown-up she had become. She no longer was a tomboy like when they were kids, but she had developed into a sexy, young, attractive woman. While they were at prom, my dad asked my mom to be with him and share their dreams together. A couple of days later they both graduated. In those days, girls either got married and started families or they became nurses. My mom became a nursing assistant and my dad started working at his law firm as an intern. That whole summer he and my mom went everywhere together.

Then one night my dad asked my mom to marry him. My mom looked at him strangely. He said, "we have been best friends since we were in diapers, and I want to spend my life with you." As he watched the tears fall down her face, he knew he had to go face my granddad to ask for her hand in marriage. As always, we would hear them talk about sports and how stuff was being run into the hole. The night grew later, and my dad asked my granddad for my mom's hand. The first thing my grandad thought was that she was pregnant. My mom looked as if she swallowed a bird. She told them no and my grandfather looked at my dad and said he knew this day would come and what took him so long?

My dad got down on one knee, took my mom's hand and asked her. As she stood there in shock, my grandmother started crying. When she answered no at first, his mouth dropped wide open.

"Why won't you be my wife?"

"I will only become your wife if you allow me to finish my schooling first."

As my mom finished school, she planned her wedding to my dad. She also noticed she was gaining weight. She was afraid to tell my grandfather, even though she was engaged. It's just not the way they did things back in the day. You got married, then you started a family. Well, my grandmother never told my grandfather that my mom was pregnant at the time of her wedding. He thought she was a virgin and till this day, he still thinks she was a virgin until their wedding night.

My mom wore a long, snug-fitting white lace wedding gown with rhinestones sewn on the collar and silver high heels. Her hair was pinned up and some of her hair hung loose from the back. She wore the same dress my grandmother wore when she got married. My dad wore a black suit, a silver shirt and his first black shoes that he brought himself. They never went on their honeymoon until months later due to their work schedule and school. Eight months later my brother De'andre was born. He weighed six pounds even and was twenty-two inches long. When mom and dad moved into their new house, they discovered my mom was with child again. It had been almost two years; dad was glad he was moving up in his office and mom had finished school and was working as a nurse in a hospital.

My little brother Isaac was born a couple of months early. My mom was working a lot of hours and not taking care of herself. She had to stop due to having pains and she had to have my brother, it was tough, and we had to go there for a few months. He weighed three pounds at birth. My parents would visit him every day in the NICU. Then one day they took my oldest brother De'andre to meet his little brother. De'andre had to be almost three at the time. Anyway, the strangest thing happened. De'andre held his hand and started singing.

His mom said it was like he looked into his eyes and got his strength to grow for De'andre. A couple of days later, they brought him home. By the time I came along, my dad owned the first law firm he ever worked at. My mom was the head nurse at the hospital. My oldest brother, De' andre Williams was going with a girl named Zola Rosado. She is from Peru, who he later on married and moved to Hawaii. They have three kids, two girls and a boy.

My little brother Isaac Williams, the loner, had a friend, but it didn't last long. He prefers to be alone. I'm excited whenever my parents decide to visit. You never know what adventure we are going to encounter. I love to see my dad and Rafael together because they play the famous "drinking game." The drinking game is to say a state, but you have to make sure you follow the alphabet. Guess who loses every year? My dad. He is the worst at this game. We always have to help him to bed after because he had too much to drink.

It's nearly Christmas. Seemed like summer had just left as I looked out the bay window thinking about different things racing through my mind. I often find myself daydreaming about different things that have happened to me. The snow is falling, and it takes me back to thinking about my childhood, playing in the snow in my front yard. It really looks icy outside, I tell myself.

Me and mama began hanging fancy Christmas ornaments on the tree. It's a great time to try for my grandson or granddaughter. I look around as if I don't hear her.

"Nice try mamita [mommy]."

"You hear me," she says and throws the pillow at me, laughing as I duck. Rafael comes in the door, "I'm home."

I walked towards him; a hug followed with a kiss. He then smiles at his mom. "When are you gonna give me and your father some grandkids?"

"As soon as you stop asking."

She says something in Spanish and leaves the room while we laugh. I got to work that next morning and I noticed something different. No one was in the front lobby.

Allison says "girl come quick Nakeya follows quickly behind her"?

"What is it Nakeya says then stops talking?" Then I see what all the talk is about. Mr. Alec Moore, an upper-class businessman from Rio de Janeiro in his forties, very handsome. A body that just leaves you breathless, eyes as blue as the sky. Staring our way, he tells us about *his upbringing. He was born in Brazil, and he comes from a wealthy family, no siblings. Sent to boarding school in the Swiss Alps known to have broken many hearts in his day. And as he is telling us a little about himself, I snap out of my little daydream. All I notice that sticks in my brain as odd is him saying, "I get what I want when I want it."*

I look as if I snapped gum in a library when he glares at me for a second, then he smiles with a devilish grin. It makes me feel strange. It seemed like he was talking to me.

"I was thinking the same thing."

"Oh, shut up, Allison. Let's go. We gotta go shopping, then get ready to go to our Christmas party."

Rafael and I will arrive about 8:00 p.m. I wore my black, tightly fitted strapless dress that flared out at the bottom and some black heels. Rafael wore a black suit with a nice red shirt that showed off his chest and some black shoes. He looked as if he walked out of a GQ magazine. My hair was freshly braided which made it really curly. Rafael's hair was neatly pulled back into a ponytail.

Alec comes over to shake our hands.

"You look great."

"Thanks. I would like you to meet my fiancé, Rafael Romas." I could tell Rafael didn't like him. Nice to meet you. I'm Alec Moore. I just bought this law firm.

They shook hands and made small talk, then Alec left. As the night went on, I noticed Alec staring at me and Rafael, while we were on the dance floor. I glanced at him, and his eyes met mine. I quickly put my attention back to Rafael. As the night went on Mr. Moore looked at us, but I just had a strange feeling whenever he would stare; he had a hungry look in his eyes. As we left, he seemed to say goodbye with his eyes to Nakeya before saying a word. He took my hand a little longer and that made me feel like he was trying to tell me something.

A couple of days later, New Year's comes and goes. Months seem to pass by. Then one evening as I'm getting ready to leave, Alec comes into my office.

"Can I help you? Nakeya asked Mr. Moore?"

"There's a very important business trip coming up, and I would like you to go Mr. Moore replied."

"Well, um Nakeya trying to find a way to get out of it"?

"It will be an overnight trip. You will be back early the very next day, but we will have to take the redeye to New York the night before Mr. Moore says quickly, he saw Nakeya trying to get out of the trip"?

"Um ok. If you promise I will be back that very next day."

"I promise Mr. Moore said."

Shaking his hand he kisses mine. Good evening, Ms. Williams.

"Good night, Mr. Moore."

As I'm driving home, I think about how Alec kissed my hand. As I'm thinking about it, I notice Rafael in the garage along with Juan and Enrique. They're working on one of the work trucks. I'm walking up and Rafael stops and kisses me.

"Yuck you're all greasy!" He laughs. I say hello to Enrique. He nods his head, then I look to Juan, who gives me a hug.

"Hola [hi] sister-in-law."

I smile. "Yeah, one day."

Rafael smiles. "Si, uno día. [Yes one day]"

I go inside and notice Rosetta putting food on the table. I gave her a hug.

"Hola [hi] baby girl, how are you?"

Drained Nakeya says in a tired voice.

She walks to the garage door and calls for the guys to come wash up and eat. I go upstairs to shower before dinner.

Hello Roman, dinner will be served in ten minutes. He nods and keeps on watching the game. I'm in the shower washing up when I hear a voice.

"May I join you?"

I smile. Why yes, sir, you may.

We start to kiss he's caressing my back. His mouth works down to my neck. Pulling him closer he makes love to me in the shower. The water is running, and I can't help but to lose myself to him completely. Every time we make love, I fall back in love with him all over again. The next morning, Allison and I went and ate at the cafe on the corner. On our way back, we noticed eyes looking at us.

"Afternoon ladies Mr. Moore says looking down at us from the lobby."

"Good afternoon, Mr. Moore Nakeya and Allison reply back being nice."

"Ms. Williams."

"Yes Mr. Moore Nakeya said with some bass in her voice"?

"Before you leave, I would like you to look over the arrangements for the business trip to New York."

I look over the arrangements quickly. "See you tomorrow evening."

"My God, you scared me. I thought you had left."

"No, I was about to leave when I saw your light on."

"I'm leaving. Going home to pack for my trip that I will be leaving for in a couple of hours."

I think of all the stuff I still have to do before I leave tonight. When I get home, I throw some clothes in my suitcase, with shoes, my underwear, and a toothbrush. Oh yeah, I need that.

Me and Rafael make love in the shower, and then get dressed.

Later on, that night, I leave and go on my business trip. Rafael drops me off at the airport. I kiss him and tell him I love him. "I will call you when I check in." As I get out of the truck, he says, "I will be waiting, mami," and kisses me again. Then he pulls off.

I enter the airport, and I see Alec looking at me. "Good evening, Ms. Williams."

"Good evening, Mr. Moore."

"Call me Alec."

We boarded the plane within minutes of my arrival. We are seated by each other as I get ready for our takeoff, he looks over. "What a lovely fragrance you're wearing."

"Thanks. Rafael gave it to me for a Christmas gift."

"It smells amazing," Alec replies."

I put on my headphones, and he smiles. I'm watching a movie and he's staring. I ignore him. Then as we get closer to the airport, he acts like he has been working on something. But in reality, he is looking at me the whole entire time. And I wonder what is he thinking? I don't care. Then I think about Rafael? How much I miss him, and it has only been two hours since we left one another. We landed in New York airport.

As I unlock my door to my room, and put my suitcases down, I make

23

my way to the phone to call Rafael to let him know I made it and that I was going to turn in for the night. The phone rings. After two times he picks up. "Hola."

"Hi."

"I love you, my love."

"I love you too, mi amor [my love] ."

"Goodnight."

"Bye." We hung up. I unpack and look for my pajamas, take a quick shower and get ready for bed. I stand under the hot water for my shower and daydream about the last time I was in the shower. I was with Rafael, and he was making love to me. When I'm done, I towel dry my hair and lotion up my body.

As I'm putting on my pajamas, the phone rings. I walk over to answer.

"Hello."

Ms. William's are you hungry Alec asked Nakeya?"

"Yes. Kinda why Nakeya says not really understanding the question?"

"Meet me in five minutes downstairs."

I hung up the phone and slipped on my denim jumpsuit, put on my slippers and unwrap my hair from the towel to air dry. I grabbed the keys off the table and went out the door. I hit the lobby, noticed Alec at the table and made my way to the table to sit down. We ordered some drinks and some food then he began to tell me about the clients we are going to meet as we wait.

I must have looked nervous because he says, "Don't be nervous. You are going to knock them dead."

"Yeah, ok Nakeya says trying not to be nervous."

Then the waitress places our food in front of us. He thanks her, but

I begin eating my shrimp scampi and sip on my glass of white wine. I finished my food and began to excuse myself to get up. "Thanks for dinner Nakeya says to Alec as she begins to get up.

"You're very welcome, Ms. Williams Alec replies with a smile."

I'm walking to the elevator and press the button when he calls me. "Na'keya."

I glance back.

"Breakfast will be served tomorrow here, approximately at seven."

"What oh yeah sure Nakeya says trying to put some distance between the two of them."

I get off the elevator, open my door to take off my clothes, and put back on my pajamas. I noticed it's almost one in the morning. I just wanted to sleep but as soon as my head hit the pillow, I was asleep.

The next morning put on my long black skirt with a red and black semi low-cut blouse along with my red pumps.

"Good morning Mr. Moore I'm ready for our meeting Nakeya says with confidence"?

He looks and comments, "You're a very sexy lady."

"Let's keep our minds on business, shall we.?"

"Yes, we shall. You look very professional this morning, Ms. Williams. We're going to meet the clients at their office."

As we are riding to the office, I'm looking at all the sights. I notice a nice store that I would like to shop at for stuff for the house, and as we turn into the building, I see a man trying to get into his car. He must have locked his keys in the car. We walk into the office and meet our clients before sitting down. In a couple of minutes, we agree on our contract, shake hands, and the next thing I know, they sign.

We are heading back to our hotel rooms to pack, and I'm in awe and disbelief. "What just happened?"

"You just signed and closed your first deal with a very high client. You should be proud. We should celebrate."

Me and Alec get a drink, or two, at the hotel bar while waiting for our flight. Rafael calls to inform me all the airports are closed till they clear the runway from ice.

"But I want to come home to you Nakeya says to Rafael, sounding like a little child."

"You will be soon Rafael says to calm Nakeya down."

I try not to be so loud on the cell with Rafael. I notice Alec looking at me as I'm talking on my cell.

"Fine, I'll wait for the airport to re-open Nakeya says."

"Like you have a choice Rafael replies half laughing." Then we hung up.

"Let's go back to the room and we'll wait there." Alec and I headed back to his room since my room was being cleaned for another guest. I sit and glance at the television and pour myself a glass of wine to settle my nerves.

"You know, you're a very beautiful woman." I look and before I can say anything, he says, "I'm a man that gets whatever I want, and I've been wanting you since I first saw you."

I stand up, and he stands in front of me, pressing me back into the couch. He then leans over to kiss me. I move my head in the opposite direction, but he draws me closer to kiss him. He begins to kiss me, and I fight at first and then I stop. His tongue caresses mine, and I give into temptation. He whispers in my ear.

Please don't, I say inside my head. My body is saying something totally different. Alec starts kissing my neck and begins to work his way down, slowly towards my breast, the television playing in the background. He is working his way to my spot. Rafael, why am I letting this man do this when I have a man who I love dearly?While I'm having a private conversation in my head. Alec begins to play with me. Closing my eyes, I imagine it's Rafael. As Alec takes his finger and circles my nipple, I breathe heavily. He starts doing different things that arouse me.

For hours, Alec does things to see what kind of reaction he can get out of me. Then, as much as I hate to admit it, I'm enjoying the different touches that Alec Moore is giving my body. He looks up, and as his eyes see my emotions on my face, he says, "don't fight the pleasure."

To take Alec's pleasure, and him knowing he has hit my hotspot, has taken my body into another level of ecstasy. That was not my intention. He noticed all of my different body languages, and with each thing he did, he noticed the changes. With each lick and suck on my clit he gave me, he would glance and see the expressions on my face. Alec knew that he was giving me pleasure. He loved knowing he had this power over me. Alec begins to move his tongue faster, making me lose my control. He carries me into the bedroom, and I kiss him, and he rubs my back.

Alec begins to put his tongue back up inside me, and I moan louder. He glances at me, smirks, then places his head back down between my thighs. Trying to take the punishment from the vibration of his tongue on my clit, I scoot closer. Alec grabs my thighs tighter. I'm starting to get that sensation, and Alec sucks and licks harder, acting like a child sucking on a lollipop. I know he can taste my sweet essence that he has released from inside coming out of me. My heart is beating so fast, it's overwhelming that tears begin to fall. I noticed the more he did this, the more I felt this tingling sensation.

I can't catch my breath even though I try to calm my heart from beating so fast. A rush, a feeling of warmth filled inside me. I had reached the end of my climax.

Alec finally stops and raises his head from between my thighs. He doesn't even notice my tears. He finds his clothes, dresses quickly, then leaves without saying a word. He left me dazed and emotional; I think. Hopefully, Alec is seeing about our flight home. I get up from the bed, quickly make my way to the bathroom, and put on the shower full blast to try and get the memory out my mind, but I just begin to sob like a newborn baby. What have I done, repeats over and over in my head. Back and forth, as this battle goes on inside my head, I'm scrubbing my body trying to get the scent of Alec and the memory of his touch out of my head.

I quickly get dressed when Alec knocks on the door. I answer, and we can start making our way back to the airport to catch our flight home. As we are boarding the plane, we sit down saying nothing to one another the whole four-hour flight. When we land, I start heading to the entrance of the airport. I notice Rafael, he looks so tired. I start walking toward him, and he is very happy to see me. I kiss and hold him so tight. "It seems like forever since I saw you," I whisper in his ear.

"I love you so much," he whispers to me. "Let's go home."

Alec must have slipped out without being noticed. I try to keep the guilty look off my face and try not to let Rafael know what had happened between me and Alec a couple of hours ago in his hotel.

I get home and I'm greeted by more family. That night, me and Rafael made love, but it felt so different somehow. As me and Rafael made love, it was full of so much passion. Where did it come from? I did stuff that I never did, and he loved every minute of the new nasty me. We woke up that next day feeling drained. I never felt this way before.

"Morning, love." Heading to the shower, I got dressed, grabbed a bagel, which I didn't even eat and headed to work. Got to work and Allison saw me.

"How was the trip Allison asked Nakeya?"

Before I could answer I heard, "Morning Ms. Williams, Ms. Bronesetti." I look at him somewhat. Morning Mr. Moore, we replied then went to our desk. During some part of the day, I started daydreaming about me and Rafael visiting my hometown, just for some of us time. As the day went on decided to call my parents. Maybe even ask them to come for a visit? I haven't seen them since the summer. If they're not on holiday they will come? Hopefully, they are not traveling to all parts of the world. They are home and they will be there in a couple of weeks. Me and Maria go get lunch. We're talking about a Mother's Day feast. Smelling the different spices and coffee. oh, my Nakeya says as she feels like she's getting sick and excuses herself quickly to the restroom. Allison is there when Nakeya comes back.

"Hey when you get here Nakeya asks, trying to reflect away from herself?"

Meanwhile Maria asks, "Are you ok Nakeya?"

"Yeah. I think I'm coming down with something, Nakeya replies?"

"I'm gone, gotta meet hubby."

"Hugs, give me kiss Nakeya as Maria leaves."

"I'll be in touch."

Allison waves. Walking back to work, Maria says, "Girl, what is wrong with you?"

"Not sure, the smell of the food and coffee never bothered me before.

Shit, I'm late."

Leaving work now, I hung up the phone. Alec comes up from behind and begins to kiss my neck. "Alec, what happened in New York was wrong, and we can't. You understand?"

"Yes," he says, but he kisses me again.

"No, no, stop." I get up from my desk a few minutes later and leave. That night I went home and dreamed about what happened in New York? I can feel Alec's hands all over me. I relived that whole night over in my dreams, not getting any sleep.

The next day at work, Alec says, "ms. Williams? May I?"

"Sure, I was just getting ready to leave."

"Alec, what are you doing?"

"You are on my mind."

"I can't do this." He feels my breast. "No, please." He sucks my nipples. "Please."

He smiles and leaves. That night, not that much sleep again, hardly any for the remainder of that week. Next week mom and dad come from Georgia and stay for a couple of weeks. I enjoyed having my mom there. The very first night they arrived, we cooked on the grill; the smell of salsa, corn, and other spices filled the air. Weeks pass by. Tonight, we are all going to our favorite restaurant because they are going back home. I can't seem to eat. I get a glass of wine, and I hardly take a sip.

"Is everything okay Rafael asked Nakeya being concerned?"

"Yes honey I'm fine Nakeya replies to Rafael but not so convincing"? Rosetta and Gloria looked at each other. A sudden smell of garlic then a strong perfume aroma came across Nakeya's nose. "Excuse me Nakeya says, rushing to the lady's room feeling nauseous. Rosetta

and Gloria look at each other again?

That's weird. It's like I can smell things like a dog can Nakeya says while talking to herself in the bathroom splashing water on her face? Nakeya returns back to the table where they finished dinner, but Nakeya doesn't eat dessert? When we get back home Rafael holds Nakeya. "Are you sure you're alright Keya" he asked her again?"

Yes I'm good Rafael Nakeya replied. Why do you ask Nakeya says walking towards him?" Before he can answer, something comes over me. I'm kissing his neck, and he hugs me tight, and he kisses my forehead while he holds me. I get on top and not sure what's gotten into me, but I just start riding him as he starts cumming. I just started grinding more.

We both drifted off to sleep. That next morning, we ate breakfast with my mom and dad, then they got ready to leave. "Take care." We all exchange kisses, and watch them get in the car and drive off. That night, I dreamt I was back in New York, and I am kissing Alec. I woke up quickly. Rafael asks if I'm okay.

"Ah, yes, just had a bad dream." I'm walking down the stairs to get coffee, feeling kinda queasy. Rosetta said, "maybe we should take you to the doctor's, yes?"

I nod, "yeah sure." This has been happening for two weeks, and I still feel awful. Rafael is happy that I'm finally going to see what's wrong with me. "Finally, you're going. Good. Call me when you get back."

"Okay."

We get to the doctors and check in. Dr. Onye asked me to get undressed, does a quick examination, and I'm finished getting dressed and waiting. As we wait, mom is saying a prayer in Spanish. Doctor Onye says, "you two are fine."

I look shockingly at her. "What do you mean? Us two?"

Rosetta looks at me. "Oh my, you are going to have my grandbaby!" She smiles, but I'm looking at the doctor.

"I'm pregnant Nakeya says, sounding shocked?"

"Yes, and I would like to get you in next week for some tests"

"Um, okay." And I cry tears of joy.

We head home, and I can't wait to see Rafael and tell him the great news. We got there and I hear him arguing with someone. "What's going on, what's wrong?" Then Juan storms out. "Please wait Nakeya says."

He turns around. "We need all the family to come over, I have good news." I serve dinner, Rafael and Juan make up, then I see outside the doorway Maria talking to her dad as he is entertaining the kids by playing a game of catch. The twins are crying. I think to myself that is going to be us in a couple of months?

"I guess it's time for Sofie and Sofia to eat?"

"Yeah they eat like pigs."

"Look who the dad is Rafael says ?" Juan then pushes Rafael which makes Nakeya laugh. Nakeya motions to everyone to get their attention"? Rafael leaves the grill,Roman stops playing with the kids. The family all begins to gather around me one by one to see what all the excitement is all about?

"What's going on Nakeya, Maria asks?"

" Yeah what is going on that is so important says Juan?"

"What's going on is that i have some news to share with the family Nakeya says happily?"

Rafael baby, you come stand by me as Nakeya reaches for his hand.

I have some great well shocking news to share?" Nakeya paused before yelling "We're pregnant!" Nakeya glanced over at Rafael. Tears start falling down his face. Rafael pulls me close. He is speechless.

"Say something Rafael, Nakeya says with a worried look on her face?"

Really Nakeya Rafael says before looking at his mom?

"Sí mi hijo, [Yes my son]" Rosetta screams to Rafael hugging Roman who is teary eyed.

He kisses me, rubs my belly, and kisses it. That next morning, Rafael is talking to my stomach. He must have thought I was asleep. He was saying how proud and excited he was. I lay there still while he kisses my stomach before going downstairs to make me breakfast. I jump into the shower, get dressed, and come down the steps. "Morning, mami [mom] Rafael says to Nakeya."

"Morning, papi [daddy] Nakeya replies back to Rafael."

"I made you pancakes," Rafael says."

"Smells good," Nakeya replied licking her lips."

"Banana blueberry pancakes with some orange-mango juice, and maple sausage patties."

Nakeya kisses Rafael as they both leave for work. "See you later babe Nakeya says getting in her car.

"I'm counting on that he replied waving as he pulled off."

The next couple of months are the hardest for me. From getting up and going to work, and not being able to keep anything down, plus the different smells throughout the house. My job with Alec didn't help. I glance in the mirror, looking at how big I've gotten. Oh my God, it seems like I got big overnight. Rafael rubs my belly, and we see the baby kick. "Papi, you see that?" He nods, then goes to brush *his teeth. "Oh yeah, next week I have an appointment. You're coming, right?"*

He looks out the bathroom door and walks over to the bed to give me a kiss. "There is no place I would rather be Rafael says."

10:30 at Dr. Onye's next week he repeats while in the bathroom gargling."

We catch a first glimpse of our little bundle of joy. We look at the screen in amazement. I feel some movement as I lay half asleep on the examination table. Rafael sings a Spanish lullaby, saying afterward, that's what your abuela [grandmother] used to sing to me.

I really enjoyed the father figure coming out of you Rafael, so sweet Nakeya says as she smiles."

Time seems to be going by so quickly now. My feet are no longer visible, and my face has gotten puffy. Closer to my due date I'll begin my maternity leave and rest for our new arrival Nakeya tells Rafael as she talks to him.

Later on, that following day Dr. Onye asks Nakeya or Rafael would they like to know what they are having?"

Yes i would Rafael says, Nakeya says no as long as it's healthy, it's not important"?

Yes, please tell me Dr. Onye Rafael says sounding eager to find out?

"Congratulations to you both you're having a girl!"

"Really it's a girl Rafael tears up as well as Nakeya."

Rafael smiles then calls Maria with the news. It's raining hard outside later on that evening and Rafael comes in and then back out with a lot of stuff he got?

"What are you doing Nakeya asks Rafael because after her appointment he dropped her off then left again while she napped?"

"You rest, mi amor [my love] , I will be there in a couple of minutes, " he replied, sounding winded coming up and down the stairs."

Rafael spends a lot more time in the spare room, and I wonder what he is doing Nakeya says to herself being curious? The next day Maria called and asked me if I felt like doing something?

"Feel like going baby shopping for my goddaughter Maria asked Nakeya?"

Rafael, Allison, Maria, and me had a blast shopping. We stopped at every store it seemed. Maria picked out so much stuff.

Are you trying to make my daughter a diva like you Nakeya asked Maria?"

"Sí [yes], like her favorite tia [auntie]."

I was laughing so hard then I felt a hard kick. Rafael looked at me.

"You, okay Nakeya as i bent over?"

"Yeah, but I think our daughter wants to come out."

That following week Maria, Rosetta, Allison, and my mom threw me a beautiful baby shower. So much stuff and so many presents. Glancing over at Rafael, I told him that I loved him.

"I love you back he replied to Nakeya.

His brothers talk to him about being a daddy. The baby kicks, and I'm even more excited. That night the family shared their baby stories. Looking over at Rafael then whispered you scared yet in his ear?

Pssh, no he said trying to be brave then says why are you?"

Nakeya swallowed hard trying to be brave but scared saying nope, piece of cake. Later on, as I look over the presents. Rafael begins looking at me then says, "Pregnancy agrees with you you're simply

35

glowing."

"Oh yeah, Nakeya replies but this morning sickness is for the birds before laughing."

Hours later Rafael says, "I'm finally done in the other room."

"Done what Nakeya says trying not to sound sleepy?"

My masterpiece come see. It's a nursery Nakeya looks shockingly around. It's so Amazing Rafael as Nakeya is still looking around holding my hands over my mouth taking in all the detail? Rafael it's beautiful there's a pink crib in the corner with a pink and purple blanket set, with all kinds of stuffed animals inside. On one wall he painted an angel to watch over her. I love it. He stands behind me and rubs my stomach.

I hope Gabriella Josafina Romas likes it."

That name Rafael, I love it, and continues to look around. He has all the clothes that we got the last couple of months already in the closet hung up and the other stuff folded into the cabinets. The changing table has Pampers and powder already set up.

"You thought of everything Rafael. Well almost he says to Nakeya."

That night Nakeya is hit with a sudden burst of energy.

You can't get enough Rafael says to Nakeya as she wants to make love nonstop."

I never get enough of you Nakeya replies, then finds another place to make love. We make love inside the bathroom, then on the bed, and ending up on the mini-love seat. He helps me back into our bed once we've showered, then we're fast asleep.

Rafael stays close to home. My due date is approaching. I awoke suddenly with a strong pain in my lower back that travels to my pelvic region.

36

"Rafael, it's time!"

"It's time he says still half asleep not understanding what Nakeya was saying.?"

"Yes time Rafael to have the baby in labor trying to be calm with the labor pains."

"Oh my when it finally kicks in, alright mami [mommy] lets go have our daughter"?

He wakes the whole house. Rafael and Roman help get Nakeya into the car. Then they drive away not that long after Rafael and Nakeya head towards the hospital. Mom and dad are following Rafael then he notices more of the family is behind them. I guess Raphael had the whole family on speed dial because it seemed like five minutes the whole family was there. Rafael gets scrubs on, and my pains get more intense. He rubs my back and I moan in pain. He kisses me. It's almost time to push. Push Nakeya, push Rafael yells as Nakeya pushes.

Nakeya reaches for Rafael's hand and continues to keep pushing. It seems like my insides are coming out, Nakeya says as she pushes. Sweating then tears fill both their eyes after they hear a small cry.

She's here Mami [mommy] Rafael says to Nakeya our daughter is here!

Gabriella Josafina Romas was born June 20, 2010, at 3:30 a.m. weighing five pounds and two ounces twenty inches long. The family walked to the nursery to see Rafael holding Gabriella up to them so they could see her before they took her for some test.

You are going to be released in a few days Dr. Onye told Nakeya."

Good Nakeya says as Rafael walks into the room hearing part of the conversation.

Rafael comes to get me and Gabby from the hospital. We get home and it's full of balloons with the family waiting to see the newest addition. The first night, Rafael took care of Gabriella. When it was time to feed her he either asked for my breast milk or he handed me Gabriella and he would watch me breastfeed her and rub her head. As she nursed, he would give me a look.

"What wrong babe Nakeya asked Rafael?"

"It's amazing, how we made love and created something so special he replies shaking his head."

It has been two weeks since I've been home. I don't feel as sore as i did a few days ago. As I'm talking to Maria, hush Nakeya says?

"What listen to your brother in the other room?"

We heard Rafael singing to Gabriella. We started laughing. He is such a good father. A few weeks go by and I'm back to work. I walked in and the whole day seemed so weird. Why do I feel like they are whispering behind my back Nakeya said to herself?

Allison comes inside Nakeya's office. Hey, girl what's new Allison says?

"What's up Allison, you tell me Nakeya, huh?"

"Girl rumor has it that you slept with Mr. Moore in New York"?

Tears fill my eyes, instantly. Oh my God. I had blocked that whole night out so much had happened that it never crossed my mind. It just happened, Nakeya says feeling the guilt all over again from that night and the other times he messed with her in the office. Which reminded her if the office realized how as i got bigger Alec would watch me but never asked if it was his from that night in New York or is that what Allison was implying was it his?

As the day went on struggled trying to get back into the swing of things after being on maternity leave? Nakeya arrived home late. As Nakeya entered the room, she could tell something was wrong.

"Mami [mommy] Rafael said in a mean sounding way"?

"I hear the baby."

"I'll go get Gabriella, Rosetta says you two talk then leaves"?

I go to give Rafael a kiss, but he moves away and then says, "you care to explain?"

"Um, explain what Nakeya says without looking at first then sees the pictures?"

"This he was really upset that his Spanish accent came out. I glanced down at the pictures he was holding.

"Let me explain it's not what you think Nakeya says trying to talk without crying"?

"Oh, really tell me what I am thinking Nakeya because I know what i see?"

"I'm so sorry. I didn't mean to hurt you.

"Did you sleep with him, mami [mommy]."

"Nakeya did you sleep with him he yells louder this time"?

Nakeya finally breaks down. I never meant for anything to happen, I'm so sorry that I hurt you Rafael, Nakeya says reaching for his hand. No Rafael please don't leave as she grabs his arm.

"Get off me Nakeya now as he pushes her off".

"I'm sorry, baby please don't go but he rushes out the door and passes Maria coming in."

Tears are running down my face. Maria comes in.

"Hey, what's going on Maria asked but Rosetta had already told her

and wanted her to come over and try to smooth things over.

"I really messed up Maria as Nakeya tries to get Rafael before he backs out"

Rafael waits, Rafael wait Nakeya screams as Rafael cries backing out the driveway fast and goes up the street".

He's gone Nakeya repeats over and over as she cries in Maria's arms. Nakeya starts talking telling her what, she doesn't say much except to give him some time to cool off, I cry more.

"One time, I drank too much, and this happens I love your brother Nakeya replies then cries."

I know and he loves you too, Maria says while holding her.

As I get myself together Maria holds her niece there's a knock at the door. Jose walks in and gives me a hug. I will talk to my little brother heard everything that happened, and we know all too well how you two are feeling right now Jose says."

I looked at Maria, puzzled how can you two possibly know how i'm feeling right now Nakeya says wiping her face.

We also had a situation like this many years ago, but we worked through it, didn't we, honey Maria says?"

"Yes we did, Jose said then kissed Maria then Gabriella"?

Still patting Gabriella to sleep, I try to sleep or at least rest my body. Mom comes in as Maria puts Gabriella in her crib then her and Jose leave.

"You will make things right, once again. I know my son and he loves you and Gabriella."

"You think so, mami [Mom] Nakeya asks?"

She hugs me then says si [Yes]. You get some rest and get your head together.

Next morning no Rafael Nakeya cries in the room looking out the window hoping to see him? The following morning Nakeya walks down the stairs and pauses when she sees Rafael's car parked in the driveway. He is holding Gabriella feeding her a bottle at the table.

I was going to breastfeed Nakeya said to break the silence.

You looked so peaceful, so I didn't want to wake you as I peeped in on you. I got here a couple of hours ago Rafael says looking at Nakeya lovingly. Mom said you tossed and turned all night and to let you rest so I did he then says as he begins to burp Gabriella who is smiling up at him. Then when I checked on Gabriella, we began playing so brought her down here to feed her. Then three hours later here you come walking down the stairs beautiful as ever.

I'll take her Rosetta says to Rafael kissing his forehead like a little boy you two talk.

I walk over to him slowly, then I lay my head on his chest. "I'm really truly sorry." Tears begin falling down my cheeks.

He holds me tight. "Mi amor, I still love you."

"Do you think we can be together again? Can we work on ourselves?"

"Sí [yes] . We can work this out, but I do have a problem. It's about your boss."

"I'll leave if I have to. I want to work on our family."

Later that night, Rafael was like a wild man. "You don't have to prove to me that you're the man. You're all I need, no one else." I started cumming, and he held me tight.

He whispered in my ear, "you are my other half which makes me whole."

"And you are my other half as well."

Gabriella begins to cry. When I go to get her, we hear dad in the nursery on the baby monitor. We then made love again, which seemed like hours. Rafael had never made me feel like he did that night. The way he had me screaming his name. Then we made our way to the bathroom to shower, and we made love again. He leaned me against the wall of the shower, opened my legs, and went inside me once again.

"You trying to make a baby? I'm all yours, papi. Fuck me harder... harder." He went harder and faster. "Oh my God! Oh my God, I'm cumming i'm cumming! Oh, papi [daddy] ." We went to bed completely drained and slept till morning.

"Mi amor [my love] Morning." He kissed me coffee Nakeya?"

Yes please she says thinking about last night in her head smiling?

"Thanks babe needed that. How do you feel Rafael smirks her way?"

I'm wonderful she says smiling and how are you, Rafael?"

"Excellente [excellent] last night was amazing!"

Allison comes around the corner and says i'm surprised Nakeya you can walk.

What are you talking about as Nakeya tries to play dumb?

Y'all nasty both Allison and Enrique say as they finish eating breakfast.

Rafael smiles when Enrique whispers something in Rafael's ear.

"Morning Rafael Allison then says smirking."

Morning Allison Rafael replies as he notices how Enrique smiles at Allison before they walk outside.

I'm gonna be late Rafael says then kisses Nakeya in the lips

See you later Nakeya he smiles.

Yes, for round two Nakeya says under her breath Rafael says Lord have mercy!

I guess you two made up Allison say sarcastically to Nakeya sipping her coffee.

Yes we did Allison over and over again most of the night.

Um girl spare me the details we could hear some of the effects from last night this morning? Nakeya asks Allison, "are you serious you could hear us? Allison doesn't answer just continues to eat?

What brings you here this morning anyway Allison you should be at work?"

You bring me here Nakeya, why me Nakeya asks Allison?

Well check on you but when I was ready to come up to your room. Enrique says, "I think my brother and Nakeya are making up if you know what i mean laughing. Then he asked me if I was hungry so we ate breakfast together then we started talking.

You two were talking, Nakeya then said Wow.

Well, you and Rafael were busy Allison says besides he's interesting and he's sexy.

I'm thinking about working from home Nakeya says as she picks at her breakfast?"

What are you serious Nakeya really Allison says almost in tears?

I can do the same thing at home that we do in the office Nakeya says besides i don't want to leave Gabriella yet?

We walk into the living room and the phone rang. Juan answers the phone, Hola. [Hello].

Hola [hello] Uncle Horace. Si [Yes], we are coming for a visit soon. Que [What]? Slow down Oh my God when did that happen? Okay, we will be there as quickly as possible. Rosetta. Mami [mommy] telephono [telephone]?

"Okay, hola [Hi] Que [what] then she replies Dio mio estaremos allí lo antes posible, Adios. [Oh my God, we will be there as soon as possible, goodbye].

I better call Rafael and break the news, says Nakeya. As soon as I got off the phone with Rafael, he said they were on their way back here then hung up. The rest of the crew starts coming in slowly, first Maria and Jose with the kids, then Rafael and Enrique coming from the back porch along with Lydia and Juan show up with the girls within minutes. As we are getting ready to tell them what happened, Rafael comes in.

Is it true, mami [mommy] about mi abuela [my grandmother] ?

Yes, It is true your grandmother is in the hospital and very sick.

We pack our suitcases and meet up at the airport. As we wait for our flight we pray trying to keep good spirits on a sad occasion. We board the plane, and we land in Argentina within six hours. We go to the big house to drop off our stuff then head over to the hospital to be with the other family members. We're greeted with hellos and hugs from the family.

Oh my God let me hold the baby one of the cousins says to Maria?

She is so cute and looks just like her daddy the other cousin says to Nakeya about Gabriella.

"Sí si [yes, yes] she does agreed Uncle Horace says then hugs Rosetta and Roman.

Look at the twins, they are getting big aunt Rosa says while wiping her eyes.

Yeah, you're telling me cousin Cruz said as he comforted Aunt Rosa.

We take turns going in to see her. We go in after Maria and Jose come out. Maria breaks down and Nakeya starts tearing up. Then Nakeya and Rafael start going into the room.

Hola abuela Josefina [Hello grandma Josefina] Rafael says trying not to cry.

Rafael mi nieto guapo [Rafael my handsome grandson] Josefina replies in a whisper.

Sí, soy yo. Te duele alguna parte Rafael asked his grandma?[Yes it's me do you hurt anywhere] ? She shook her head no then closed her eyes.

She had to be in her late nineties. Then Josefine looks at Nakeya

Hola Nakeya ¿Cómo estás querida? [Hello Nakeya, how are you doing dear] then Nakeya replies

Hola, señora cómo se siente, ¿me alegro de verla de nuevo? [Hello ma'am how are you feeling nice to see you again]

Josefina replies to Nakeya, He estado mejor pero es lindo ver a mi familia, then smiles.[I have been better but it's nice to see my family]

She talks for hours and hours. We show her the great grandkids. Gabriella, Sophie, and Sophia.

¿Cual es el nombre completo de Gabriela? [What is Gabriella 's full name] Josefina asked Rafael?

Gabriella Josefina Romas Rafael says as she smiles than tears up

She repeats her name Gabriela Josefina Romas?

Yes our daughter is named after you.

Eso es tan dulce [That's so sweet] she says then kisses Rafael.

We're getting ready to say goodbye for the night.

The next thing we know the doctors are rushing into her room. Rosetta just breaks down Roman and Jose rushes to her side to comfort her. Grandma Josefina was coughing then more people rushed by with carts. Lydia looks at me that's not good?

We're sitting in the waiting room. How is she Doctor when we saw him come around the corner?"

Rosetta and Roman stood as we were still seated looking at his reaction. I'm sorry we have done all that we could, but she did not make it.

Rosetta screams and Roman just holds her. Nakeya cries in Rafael's arms. We go back into the house, it's so quiet we don't say much. Rafael starts telling stories then pretty soon others share their stories about their grandma. Nakeya goes to lay the baby down and gets ready for bed. Rafael grabs a drink. I go over and hug him and tell him I'm here if you need me?

I'm glad and sat on his lap hugging him.

A couple of days later we buried Josefina in the family cemetery. Alongside her parents but also next to her late husband Ernesto. He was a hundred when he died. As the service ended the mariachi band played all the way back to the house. We cried then shared more stories about Josefina. We left a few days later. Rafael gives the keys to the house to her son Ernesto Jr. Ernesto Jr placed a box in Rafael's pocket and said nothing on our way back home. I'm wiped out and put the baby in the crib, grabbed the baby monitor and within minutes fell asleep.

Reached over to feel for Rafael he's not there? He must be downstairs. Checked on Gabriella still sound asleep. Mom and dad are watching tv or shall I say, watching them. Eased the door close tip toed downstairs. Rafael is drinking Jose Cuevo and he's really feeling it.

You okay honey Nakeya asks Rafael, but he just stares at first?"

He looks at me drunkenly and says come here Nakeya? He starts taking my clothes off.

Honey let's go to bed she says then she tells him to stop? Stop you're hurting me, Rafael?

Not even ten minutes later he comes staggering in the bedroom. He pulls the blanket down and pulls up my nightgown. Roughly we made love. I wanted to say stop but I didn't. He falls asleep holding me like usual. That next morning, he tells me I'm sorry mami [mommy]. I hurt you, I don't know what got into me. It won't happen ever again."

He goes to work and an hour later the doorbell rings. Delivery for Ms. Nakeya. Its flowers read the card and it says sorry for last night, much love, Rafael. They smell so good.

I can't believe Gabriella is six months and crawling everywhere. All you hear is no, Gabriella, no mami. But if I hear Gabriella Josafina Romas she's in trouble.

"What's in the box?"

"You'll find out soon enough."

Soon as Rafael gets home, Gabriella holds her hands out for her daddy. She is such a daddy's girl. Well, tonight Rafael must have been in a good mood. "Hola, I'm home."

"Shh, the baby is asleep." He kisses me sweetly.

How are you feeling? Hey, Maria, Allison."

Hey, what's up?

Look at her, she is getting so big.

Yes, I know."

I miss you at work.

Really can't say I miss the office.

Alec Moore left suddenly. Rumor has it that he is getting sued for, listen to this sexual harassment?

What Nakeya says like she's shocked? From who asked Maria?

Tina Scott from the mailroom Allison says while snacking on some popcorn on the table.

Yes, he supposedly asked her out and when she said no, he began making sexual jokes about how big her butt was and how he wanted to touch her big boobs.

Wow drama so much drama at the office.

So how have you been Nakeya really, Allison asked her?

Maria is playing with Gabriella not paying us any mind. Gabriella laughs and pulls auntie's hair.

So do you want to go back?"

"Not really. I like working from home. I can cook, clean, do laundry and most importantly spending time with my baby girl.

It's almost Christmas time again, can't believe it's almost been a year since Grandma Josefina passed away?

February 12, 2010, the world lost a special woman in my opinion.

Hey bro Maria tells Rafael.

Hey sis he replied back giving her a high five.

Where is Jose he asked her?

Home with the kids playing dress up but you didn't hear that from me"?

Tell him hey sure will.

Got to go have to make dinner.

Call you later about Christmas.

Hey, honey, how are you?

"*Fine, now that I'm home with my two favorite ladies. Rosetta clears her throat. I meant to say three. My three favorite ladies. He grabs Gabriella and kisses her.*

Hola Mamita [Hi Mommy] Rafael says to Rosetta.

Rafael como estas mi hijo? [How are you son]

What are we going away for Christmas this year?

We are going to Disneyland Rafael says to Nakeya!

Disneyland really Rafael the whole family Nakeya asked?

Rafael kissed Nakeya before saying yeah the whole family. I have a surprise for everyone?

We left the day before Christmas Eve. Ready to go

off to Disneyland we go. Sophia and Sophie are a year old now walking really well. We all started boarding the plane and had not noticed Enrique. Where is Enrique, Nakeya asked while sitting next to Rafael?

He is already there Rafael says he left last night he's helping me with my surprises? Come to daddy Gabriella then he asks her do you want a brother or sister? You want one of each he replies then looks at Nakeya? Nakeya turns away making pretend to not hear what he's saying? We get off the plane. How far is the hotel Jose asked because I'm ready to get in some water?"

No hotel we are going to our family vacation house Rafael says.

Our vacation house Nakeya says in a surprised tone?

Yes, I brought us a house. Whenever we come here, no more reservations.

Oh, Rafael, that's why I love you.

Oh no there is more. That's only one of the four surprises.

Surprises I'm too old for surprises.

We pulled up to this big house with a porch and a pool in the back. It has six bedrooms, three bathrooms and a finished basement. For less than a thousand dollars a month if we rent it out if not here to make extra money. My client, who I was doing landscaping jobs for, said that since I helped build his new house, he would sell me one of his older homes.

I fell in love instantly. Each room had its own theme. Wow you really have been keeping busy. That night, we started getting the decorations and other Christmas stuff together. We sang Christmas carols. Out pops Enrique sings It's A Small World.

Enrique brings out the Eggnog?

Sure, that sounds great.

We all gathered around the big table. Rafael is feeding Gabriella. Nakeya where was the first place I took you in Argentina?

A little saloon not sure of the name we had some coronas and tequila shots. Jose and Enrique bring out two shot glasses. What in the world looked down and saw a ring.

I opened my mouth, and nothing came out. The promise I made to you on Nana's death bed in Argentina? That i'm going to make an honest woman of you? He gets down on one knee, and I really start crying Na'keya you and I have been through a lot, and you have been there whenever I needed you. Gave me my first of our many kids to come? The family laughs and Nakeya just looks shocked. I loved you the first time I saw you in Argentina, and love you more each and every day. Nakeya will you do, he cries will

you give me the honor and pleasure of becoming mí esposa [my wife] ?"

"Sí, sí [yes, yes] I would love to be your esposa [wife]"!

He gets up and we exchange a passionate kiss along with a hug. The family is clapping and congratulating us on our engagement. Sister-in-law welcome to the family officially. I wipe my face. "Mommy, Daddy and showed my parents the ring.

When did you get here?

I couldn't ask you to be my wife without your parents. Without them there would not have been you.

Son welcome to the family and my dad shook his hand.

That night, Gabriella stayed in the room with my parents. I shake my head. I can't believe we're engaged?

Well believe it Mrs. Rafael Juan Romas.

I turned to him, "I like the sound of that."

Kissing his neck, he leaned his head back and slowly we rocked back and forth. He rubbed my back. I arched my back, and he went farther inside. I'm getting hot, moaning louder and enjoying the pleasure that both his mouth and penis were giving me. Please don't," but I really want him to keep doing it. I start to shake, and he holds me to stop from shaking.

The kids fell asleep and as they slept, we put their presents and other gifts under the tree.

I have all that I need on my finger and in the crib and most importantly right next to me. We all turned in and got ready for the big Christmas morning breakfast. The kids had a ball. So many toys, they played for hours.

A week later New Years approached us. Are you ready for your third surprise?

He hands me an envelope addressed to Mrs. Romas.

Open it Nakeya he says.

To my surprise it's a honeymoon for the Virgin Islands. Oh my God Rafael love you so much. But you already knew that.

Your final surprise will be on New Year's Eve?

Can't wait.

"Na'keya,Na'keya yes Jose are you okay in there?"

Yeah, I'm good but I have a little surprise of my own to tell your brother.

No, are you really again?

Yes really, I just took another test in the bathroom.

Wow congratulations, that is great news.

Congratulations on what Rafael says.

Oh, hey boo you scared me. Um well we're expecting again.

We're gonna have a baby!

"We're gonna have a baby!

Quiet you gonna wake the dead.

Oh yeah lucky me morning sickness?

I think when we get back, we should get Gabriella baptized."

Yeah, and make a doctor's appointment," Raphael says rubbing my tummy.

Dinner is good.

"Yeah, it was good."

Can we have some Hoover?

Maria is really funny Nakeya says as she throws a pillow at her.

So, Jose, how would you and Maria like to be godparents to Gabriella Josafina Romas? Juan and Lydia would you give us the honor of being godparents of our newest addition?

Seriously bro of course yes what an honor.

The brothers are hugging and it's so sweet. New Years is almost here countdown 10,9,8,7,6, 5, 4, 3, 2, 1 Happy New Year.

I love you so much Keya.

I love you more Rafael. The room is filled with so much love. Enrique is getting close to Allison and seems to be giving up his player's card.

Home sweet home, Maria?

Hey, can we get together and make plans for this baptism?

"Yeah, sounds great."

Okay, love you.

Love you too."

Yeah, that's a big mouth Maria.

Hey sis, love you too.

You sure about having the baby?

"Yes, why wouldn't I be?"

Gabriella is six months, and the baby will be born in August.

Oh my God.

What?

My wedding and pregnancy we have to start making plans where do we begin?

Yes, let's start planning this wedding that ring is beautiful.

Yes, it is it was my mother's passed down through the generations.

Josefina's?

Sí [yes], she gave it to Rafael at the hospital along with her blessings.

This dress is cute Nakeya look Allison said.

Nah too plain for me, Nakeya replied.

What about this one Nakeya, Lydia pointed to?"

Nah too ugly Maria said, i was asking Nakeya not you?"

Maria will you be my Maid of Honor?"

Yes, I thought you would never ask.

You know you make my brother happy he really loves you. You have changed him Nakeya.

Changed him how Maria, Nakeya asked?

Well, you met him in Argentina he lived here but left.

Really, he never told me why he leave?"

He was asked to be in the gang, and he left when he refused to join. Rick, his friend from school, had gotten into the wrong crowd. Long story short the gang tried to kill him.

Wow I'm glad he did leave but he never told me."

It's for my god baby how much do I owe you? Okay out of fifty. Thank you please come again come let's go? Hey, you okay Nakeya you don't look so good?

No think I should go home and lay down.

Okay let's get you home."

Thanks girl again had some fun before i started feeling like this.

Thanks, see you later don't worry I will finish making the arrangements.

Nakeya where are you, Rafael started calling her in the hallway.

Hey baby, why are you laying down?

When you get here Rafael half sleepy? You okay Nakeya?"

Just a little tired and a bit dizzy, nothing serious that's all.

You sure because you look pale and you're shaking?

Um yes i just feel really dizzy.

Oh God Nakeya, baby you okay? Oh god my poor Keya. Rafael yells for his mom to call 911.

Rafael, it hurts so bad Nakeya starts crying in Rafael's arms.

It's okay help is coming as he rubs her belly?

Oh no Rafael? What Nakeya i don't want to lose the baby Rafael?

I'm here Nakeya just try to calm down.

I'm scared Rafael, calm down Nakeya.

I'm here, I'm here Na'keya we will see what's going on.

Excuse me, Mr. Romas, my name is Dr Jin we ran some tests, and both your wife and baby are fine.

Oh, that's good news, that's a relief.

Na'keya was just having Braxton hicks, false labor it happens sometimes she's having them a bit earlier than normal, so i want to keep Nakeya overnight just to keep an eye on her?

Okay things are fine back at home Maria has Gabriella. You just rest Nakeya and know I will be right here.

How are the plans coming along Maria?

They are all done Nakeya told you I got this.

Really all the planning and arrangements all done.

Yes, the baptism of Gabriella will happen in a couple of weeks.

I'm so sorry I didn't get to help you with the planning.

You just rest Nakeya and concentrate on getting better afterwards so we can work on your wedding plans.

Hey nice to see you up and about Rafael says to Nakeya.

Yeah, the first couple of days back home were sort of hard, but I don't have those pains anymore.

A few weeks past and we start to go inside the church for the baptism. Oh, my Maria these decorations are Amazing great job.

The church is so beautiful you picked the best church.

Father Lopez, I want you to come and meet my family i was telling you about.

Good evening you must be Rafael and Nakeya? My parents Rosetta and Roman then nods to the others. Well look at this bundle of joy this must be Gabriella, shall we get started?

As the service is going on Nakeya must have zoned out. What is her name?

Oh, it is Gabriella Josefina Romas. These are her godparents Maria and Jose Gomaz.

I have now baptized Gabriella Josefina Romas your godchild.

Gabriella cries as he sprinkles water on her head.

Later back at the house the phone rings and Rafael slams it down.

You, okay? Nakeya asked him being concerned."

Yes, excuse me for a minute Nakeya?

Rafael is talking to Juan and his whole body just changed from earlier after that call.

What scares me is that look in his eyes, what's that for?

They will not take me away from my family.

Nakeya overhears Rafael whispering to Juan as she approaches. Hey, you guys' time to eat but Nakeya doesn't push the subject about what she overhears.

Sure, Rafael then tells Juan we will talk later.

Rafael is there anything going on Nakeya asked what's wrong?

I will take care of its Nakeya; Rafael kisses her and says let's eat?

Later that night while laying inside his arms it always makes me feel safe.

Rafael and Juan left early that following morning before I got up?

Enrique, have you seen your brother?

Earlier I did he was going with Juan?

Did he say where he was going with Juan, Nakeya asked?"

Only to tell you not to worry he will be back soon.

Hours later they walk into the front door Rafael where have you been, Nakeya asked?

Ouch why did you hit me Nakeya? We had to take care of some things in Argentina.

Things like Nakeya says trying to understand why all the secrecy.

We got a phone call to hear the reading of Grandma Josefina's will. She must have changed it she left each of us something and got it notarized before she died.

Really there is something even for our new baby Nakeya? How did she know we would have another baby Nakeya said being amazed?

Well, it states who gets what and when they are to receive it. Maria and Jose, you got the deed to her house in Argentina?

Oh, wow we love that place, thanks Grandma Josefina. There's more Rafael says as he continues to read the contents of the paper.

Your kids get two thousand each when they turn eighteen. Lydia and Juan? You get four thousand for the kids when they turn eighteen, and a vacation spot in Argentina City."

She had property in Argentina City?

Yes, Rosetta Romas I mean, Mom you get her family albums and continue to record the birth of kids born into the family, the recipe books, and four thousand dollars. You will have to call I have got all the numbers.

Nakeya and I after we get married will gain the newest property in Argentina. In her will she said, she purchased it last year after the birth of Gabriella it's a four-bedroom house to my precious Gabriella, wish I would have known you more she will also receive three thousand dollars at the age of eighteen and to the new baby three thousand.

I never knew Grandma had that much money Juan says.

Me too, Enrique says as he shakes his head.

The following day the ladies go to the store dress shopping for Nakeya's wedding. Maria and Allison, what do you think Nakeya says as she models her first gown?

No girl it's too dull for you they replied then Nakeya tries on another one?

Okay, what about this one?

Like the top Maria says, not the bottom Allison replies back.

Okay, what about this one?

Nah maybe it's time for another store they say to Nakeya next shop.

Okay off to the next shop then all three of them leave and walk a block to the next shop.

By the time you find one you will need a bigger size Allison blurts out.

Yeah, don't remind me Nakeya says as she rubs her stomach smiling.

How is your morning sickness Maria asked Nakeya as they look for options for her to go try on?

Not as bad this time Rafael has it, mostly thank goodness for that.

My poor brother Maria says as they tell Nakeya to go try them on.

What about this one Allison spots by the back and hands it to Nakeya?

Oh my God that's the one Allison, Nakeya and puts it on? Nakeya looks at herself in the mirror. It's a strapless off-white ball gown with a floor length veil so beautiful it's so you we both agree.

Now for the Maid of Honor and Bridesmaids gowns yeah Allison says.

Nah nah Nakeya it's not speaking to me Allison says as she continues to look. Yes, this one Nakeya, Allison says happily.

Nah nah don't fit Maria says. Yes, this is the one Nakeya, Maria smiles.

Where are the guys trying on suits Nakeya? Yeah, we have to meet them in twenty minutes.

Are you guys ready?

Yes, hello baby boy you guys found your suits?"

Yes, because men unlike you ladies have too many things to look at designer, color, form?

Sure, you didn't have the same problems as us, no because if we look good in it, we take it?"

Well, all we need is a wedding date Rafael, how about May? May is good Juan says?

Nah Nakeya speaks up I will look like a blimp?

You will still be the prettiest bride to me, Rafael says.

Ahh so sweet Allison says then Juan follows up with saying to Nakeya and Rafael watching you two being so in love and, kissing

you're gonna make me puke.

Shut up Juan, Rafael says as he hits him on his arm which makes him laugh.

What about on June 21 Lydia says as she looks at her calendar?"

No Nakeya says quickly why would you say June 21st it's too close

Gabriella's first birthday?

I can't wait any longer for Rafael to stop eating. I want to make you Mrs. Rafael Juan Romas? A few weeks later, we are celebrating again.

Happy Valentine's Day Nakeya, Rafael screams to her in the other room.

Rafael, I can't hear you still in the shower, be out in a minute.

Oh, Rafael it's gorgeous oh my goodness, Rafael. It's so beautiful.

It's a locket with a sonogram of the baby and on the other side a picture of Gabriella when she was little.

We should go, we have reservations for eight.

Where are we going anyway Rafael, Nakeya you have to wait?"

It's a surprise that's why but know that everyone will enjoy it.

We get there and Maria and Jose, Juan and Lydia, and Enrique and Allison have already been seated.

Since when has Allison and Enrique been a couple Nakeya says?"

For a couple of months Allison replies to Nakeya and we're going strong Enrique added.

You didn't tell me Allison; how come I am supposed to be your girl?

Allison says you are my girl, but we wanted to keep it hush hush trying to see what could develop.

I think it's great maybe you will settle down yet Rosetta says.

Maybe Enrique is the one Allison, Nakeya says? Dinner was great and so was the company.

How is work going, Nakeya asked Rafael as they lay in bed talking.

Slow but don't worry, work will pick up in a few weeks?

"I can go back to work Rafael to help with the bills," Nakeya says.

No Nakeya I want you to be home with the kids and take care of the home?

You sure maybe just a part time job then to help, Nakeya replied?

Good night, we will talk about it more later on alright you rest.

Night Na'keya, night Rafael i love you so much you know that.

Hey Daddy's, little girl is getting big so is your mom? Hey i heard that Nakeya says.

I just came back from the doctors and got some new sonograms?

I want to see them Rafael says sorry I couldn't come this time.

Look sucking on his or her thumb still too early to know the sex? Ah butt shot, ahh they are looking up and gained three pounds Rafael.

You're still sexy Nakeya then we see Enrique. What's going on?"

"I'm gonna ask Allison to marry me?

What that's great news.

Congratulations wow you're gonna come off the market?

I'm so glad you are going to finally settle down Rosetta says."

I'm going to ask the question tonight at dinner.

Here Nakeya asked that was the plan so the whole family would be here Enrique replied?

Well, this calls for something special Rosetta says. I know just the thing Na'keya replied. So, you two will help me right Enrique says?

Sure, no problem come Nakeya we have work to do before tonight?

Gabriella is getting big huh, bro?

Yeah and now, we're getting ready for our wedding, another baby and now your wedding?

Did someone say wedding?

Yes, hey Maria, hey Jose the kids are in the basement playing.

Where is Juan and Lydia?

They are coming had to pick up some things for mom but just think the kids will be turning one soon.

Yeah, I know are they planning a party? So will my god baby little Gabbie. Give her to me, no you wait?

"Where's Na'keya?"

In the kitchen cooking with mom.

Hey Jose, hey Nakeya what are you feeding my girl?

Juan and Lydia hey y'all sorry we're late.

Dinner is almost done.

I will get the family Rafael says to Nakeya.

Where is Allison, Maria says?

I'm right here Maria just had to go steal a kiss from my Gabbie.

Well Mom and Nakeya dinner was great Enrique says as he holds his hands for Allison.

Allison, yeah Enrique, I have something to ask you.

Allison, we have been together for four months, and you have changed me."

I'll say Rosetta says out loud making the family laugh.

And will you marry me Allison and become my wife?

Oh Enrique, yes Allison replied I will become your wife!

Welcome to the family officially Allison we all said.

Gee thanks Allison says well Na'keya we will be sisters after all laughing.

That night Rafael gets on top, and he goes inside me. He kisses my neck while playing with my nipple with his fingers teasing me. I can't help but move closer into each pump moaning from ecstasy. Love you Nakeya so much.

I love you too Rafael, you make me feel so good.

Taking all of him inside me we can feel our little one move inside. I think about how much he means to me and start the day we met.

The twins will be turning old soon and we're going over Lydia's and Juan's house to talk about their party.

Later that afternoon hey babe where are the twins?

Sofia is getting changed and Sofie is walking somewhere?

Hey baby girl you are getting so big.

Hey everyone's in the back either in the pool or on the deck?

Hey, you are getting big Nakeya, Maria says.

Hello Allison and Enrique or should I say future sister-in-law?

Not yet Allison says but then Enrique says it's close enough?

Happy birthday to you, Happy birthday to Sophie and Sophia Happy Birthday to you.

Wow look at those cakes they're beautiful but why two?

The kids got so much stuff tonight, do you agree Rafael?

Yeah, they did but they have so much in common but not it's weird.

I'm gonna lay Gabbie down she played herself out.

Hey, did mom seem a little distant Nakeya asked Rafael?

Yeah, I guess we are making her feel old with all these grandbabies?

No, she seemed preoccupied with something serious on her mind.

Well I overheard them talking saying something in Spanish and i don't know that much.

I will ask and see if something is wrong in the morning, alright?

Night mi amor [my love]. Rafael says to Nakeya.

Night mi corazon [my heart] Nakeya replies to Rafael.

Rafael says to Roman Papi algo mal [Daddy something wrong]?

Roman replies no pasa nada estoy bien. [nothing is wrong i'm fine]

Rafael says ok but I don't think he believes his Dad. Come let's eat

Rosetta says.

Dinner was great as usual Mommy and Nakeya.

We find out what we're having tomorrow Nakeya says breaking the odd silence.

What do you want this baby to be Rafael, Nakeya asked him?"

It doesn't matter as long as it's healthy, a son would be great. Rafael winks at Roman.

I will put in the order for the big man to make that happen son.

Nakeya and Rafael welcome please sign in and the Dr will see you.

Dr. Onye afternoon you two it's been a while, so tell me Nakeya

How are you feeling?

Good Gabriella is walking now Nakeya says so i don't have to hold her as much.

Oh, you are gaining at a slower rate this time. It's fine she says just make sure you eat whenever you can or snack? Do you want to know the sex of your baby?"

Yes, we do Rafael says really excited to know the sex. Nakeya says

Rafael but I don't Nakeya says?

Yes Dr. Onye please tell me, Nakeya you can wait outside?

Congratulations Mr. Romas, you are having a son?

What did I hear you right we're having a son? He will be Rafael junior.

Maybe looking at Nakeya's reaction not so much, thank you Dr. Onye.

You're welcome, see you in a few weeks and make your next appointment before you leave?

We are having a boy Nakeya my son, then Rafael says our son babe.

Watch out Enrique your turn? It will happen, Rosetta says with a smirk.

Lydia, we have to make a boy, Juan says to Lydia trying to kiss her.

Only if you are carrying it Juan, Lydia replies, and we busted out laughing.

Happy Mother's Day to my beautiful future wife, mother of my kids.

Wow Na'keya, you look like you're ready to pop Maria says. She's gonna blow."

Shut up, Jose for I hurt you Nakeya says jokingly.

Hey guys how's everyone doing?

Where is everyone, they are all outside?

I have to go get fitted for my gown again Nakeya says.

Again, why is it because you are nervous about fitting it?

I'll go there first then go get stuff for Gabriella's birthday.

Hey is everyone here Maria asked?"

Everyone is here except Lydia, Jose replied.

Okay she already knows the news?"

Knows what news, what does Lydia know that i don't?"

Allison is pregnant, Nakeya blurts out.

What are you serious Rosetta says to Maria?

Allison says and we picked a wedding date August 18?

Where's it going to be Allison as Rosetta rubs her belly?"

Where going to get married In Argentina, Enrique finishes.

What really wow that will be so beautiful.

Rafael, you are your own boss, you don't need to worry about leaving.

True but I still have to get my assistant to cover for it, which won't be a problem.

Congratulations again Enrique, you're growing up little bro.

Well Allison, are you excited about being pregnant, Rosetta says you haven't said much?

Do you want kids, or you don't want kids talk to tell us we're family?"

I wanted to concentrate on one thing at a time now it's two.

Lydia, you finally made it so come join us, we're talking to Allison.

A couple of weeks have passed so are you all ready to go back to Argentina?

It's so beautiful there and we can check on our house while we're here?

The one in Florida is being rented out and they are such a nice family?

The Grant family have four kids, two of each, and have been married for ten years.

"Mom and Dad, your 50th Anniversary is coming up.

Please don't make a fuss, Rosetta says.

Too late Jose says we're planning something big. Across the town

Hey Mrs. Williams, hello Ms. Rich, I'm here to make some alterations to my dress.

Come put it on then Ms. Rich says to Nakeya oh my?

What's wrong Nakeya says about to cry? We have to take it in a bit."

Take it in are you serious thought you were going to say take out.

You have lost a couple of inches around your stomach area.

You're eating right Nakeya, Maria asked as she sits down?"

Yes Maria, Nakeya replied like a horse sometimes.

You want me to take it in Ms. Williams, it's up to you?

No leave it you never know i might gain some weight before my wedding.

I'll keep checking how long til the big day?

Three weeks Nakeya says but it's Gabriella's birthday today.

Oh my God time has flown by I remember when you were pregnant.

Rafael, what are you doing?

That's enough, one more Nakeya just one more maybe two?

Rafael stops hogging the baby, you can see her all the time.

Shut up Maria, like you haven't seen her in years?

Hey, you look like you have gained some more weight Allison?

We will find out tomorrow at the doctors. Mom and Dad, how are you?

We're good and excited about all this great news we keep hearing.

"So, you think you got enough Rafael?"

Yes, I do just want to make Gabriella's day special.

Wait until our son is born Rafael says?

Mr. Romas, shall we sing it in Spanish Nakeya askes Rafael?"

No in English Nakeya it's fine she doesn't care all she sees is things to mess with.

Happy birthday to you, happy birthday Gabriella Josefina Romas. Happy birthday to you. Then later on that evening the family leaves.

Sweet dreams my little baby girl.

"Shh she's wiped out she had a very busy day. Rosetta yells for Rafael?

"Rafael, Rafael come quick downstairs please hurry?

It's your dad and I need you to help get him up off the floor.

Dad, how did you fall, were you feeling dizzy or what happened?

Nakeya comes down the stairs and sees Rafael helping his dad up off the floor. Oh, my Roman, are you ok Nakeya pouring him a glass of water?

Yes, just lost my balance again he says then he stops talking.

Again, so this happened before Rafael looked more concerned?"

A few weeks ago, while doing some work out back. Dad I will take care of the lawn or Jose, Juan even Enrique.

Hey what's going on Juan comes in the door dropping off something Nakeya left?

Dad fell and then Rafael says this is not the first time either.

Papi [Daddy] why didn't you say something are you sick or your legs.

"I'm okay," Roman says as he drinks his water and catches his breath.

Can you talk to him? He won't listen to me then I will tell Maria.

Don't tell Maria, Roman says all she will do is worried?

Don't tell me what? Papi [Daddy] fell twice? Roman, are you okay?

That following Thursday we all yell Happy Anniversary to them.

Happy Anniversary Mom and Dad, Rafael says.

What should we do first Nakeya says to Rosetta getting her coat?

You have a day at the spa with just us girls Nakeya says then they go towards the door.

We're ready to leave you got Gabby right?

Yes Keya, go have fun with Mom and we will meet up with you all later.

Bye you guys, the ladies say as they leave out the front door.

Hey Allison, you're late come on girl let's go.

Hey guys, I'm coming hold up had to kiss my baby?

Dad, we also have a big day planned for you, Juan says.

I'm fine Roman says you can stop looking at me, the babysitter is here.

Let's go gentlemen, we have a lot to do before we meet up with them.

Wow, Roman says haven't been here since you three were kids.

We know so enjoy it's your anniversary we will have three beers please.

You mean four Jose can't you count Juan says joking with him?

No Roman says may I have a shot of tequila in a cold glass?

Okay Dad your grown so the waitress says four beers, two nachos and a cold shot of tequila? Coming right up, when we were finished, we did some shopping and headed back home to change.

We're back, Maria yells to let the guys know that it was time for the second part.

Hey, you have fun with the ladies, I did. Did you with the guys, sure did.

We saw a boxing match and what about you, Rosetta where you go.

70

A very relaxing day at the spa and got my feet and nails done.

Ladies, are we ready? You look beautiful like the first time I saw you Roman says to Rosetta.

Let's eat, we are starving, everything looks great. We thank you all.

We all pitched in for this gift so please follow us into the living room.

You have gifts to open so please sit down and start opening them.

"Thank you, guys, so much for the lovely day and the dinner. Gifts mean so much to me and your dad. Gracias [thank you].

Rafael we are going to be late, no we're not go ahead.

Gabriella is getting her diaper changed.

Dr. Onye, it's nice to see you again.

How are you three doing?

Just fine, we're just waiting for his arrival so I can hold him.

Nakeya how are you feeling any issues?

I feel like a whale trapped in a skinny suit.

Well, you have gained ten pounds since your last visit and the baby boy weighs around six maybe seven pounds.

Gabriella was so much smaller Nakeya says.

It's your big head Rafael, Nakeya says.

Boys tend to be bigger than girls, Dr. Onye said for Rafael's sake.

Gee Rafael remind me to kick your ass later, Nakeya shakes her head.

You want to see your son you two, here he is his vitals are good.

Well, you have dilated three centimeters will see you in a week unless you deliver Dr. Onye says.

Mom and Dad were home. Anyone home are you upstairs?

Hey how's our grandson doing? Is he getting big?

Growing like a weed Rafael says then ducks because Nakeya threw a pillow at him.

Good, nice to hear you're going to have a healthy baby boy.

Allison, you okay you're looking pale Rosetta says, morning sickness. Nakeya come here. Surprise! You threw me a baby shower Rafael?

Everyone is outside enjoying the weather. Looks like rain.

Enrique just saying looks like rain hope not.

Wow thanks everyone for coming again celebrating the birth of our son Kaden.

Nakeya how are you feeling sorry we surprised you, but we thought you found out?"

Ready to evict little Kaden i can't rest or lay down or walk?

You're gonna breastfeed Kaden, Nakeya?"

Yes, it will make me lose weight faster. Been thinking about starting my own business? Been trying to get in touch with my dad to see if he knows any good realtors.

Oh yeah for office space with a nice size parking lot maybe room for a daycare in case I have to take little man to work.

How does my brother feel about you going back to work?

Haven't talked about it yet. Maria hope he doesn't mind.

What shouldn't I mind Na'keya he asked?

Well, I was gonna talk about it later after the baby is born. I was going to start my own law firm. Before you say no work from home three days to take care of the kid's shorter hours.

The music is loud. People are dancing. It's finally cooling down. Roman and Jose are talking about business plans. Rafael and Juan are playing with Sophie and Sophia in the pool. You can smell the hamburgers on the grill, macaroni and cheese. Everyone is having fun. Trying to get around talking to people.

Thanks everyone for the baby gifts, we really appreciate it.

Tonight, has been full of surprises Nakeya says this baby shower.

Well, if you want to go back to work, Nakeya you know I support you just don't overwork yourself.

That's why I love you Rafael, you always have my back.

It's my job to please you Nakeya and make sure you're happy.

Rafael sometimes I have to thank the man above that you stayed. Oh, my felt a bit dizzy and my pajamas are wet. Think my water just broke Rafael?

You sure Nakeya maybe the water bottle cap is not screwed tight?

Let me check then collapsed on the floor. Rafael picks her up and takes her to the car and drives to the hospital. He calls Dr. Onye to tell her what happened and will meet them there. Nakeya wakes up in the hospital.

Dr. Onye is calling her to see if Nakeya is alert?

Mrs. Williams, Na'keya how are you feeling checking her vitals.

Where is Rafael, Nakeya asked why am I here, what happened?

Rafael is changing into some scrubs and the baby is under stress. We have to do an emergency c-section?

I'm scared Rafael, Nakeya I'm right here it's going to be alright?

It's so bright in here can't see anything, concentrate Nakeya?

Nakeya count backwards starting from ten, Dr. Onye says.

Ok Dr. Onye ten, nine, eight then nothing just her breathing.

Nakeya, can you hear me Dr. Onye says to Nakeya no answer?

She's out, Dr. Onye then tells the assistant to watch her vitals?

Let's begin scalpel Rafael looks as they begin cutting, then the doctor yells need suction, clamp, pass me some big gauges. Then there is a faint cry.

He's here Na'keya, Rafael tries to wake her up our son is here.

She's under a mild sedative she'll be groggy for a few hours. Mr. Romas wants to know his weight? Seven pounds three ounces and twenty-four inches long full of hair.

Excuse me sir, we have to take him for some tests and bring him back in a few. Do you have a name yet for this little handsome man?

Yes, his name is Kaden Ivan Romas. I will put it on the front of his bed.

Thank you, sir and Congratulations, on the birth again.

Hours later they bring Kaden back into the room where Nakeya is somewhat awake but still groggy.

Where's Kaden, Nakeya says in a sleepy voice, "can i get something to drink?

Kaden is in my arms. Would you like to see our handsome son?

Yes, I would oh my god all that hair, handsome like his Daddy?

How are you feeling mi amor [my love] Rafael asked Nakeya?

Sore very sore Rafael, he's perfect and look at those cheeks?

There is a knock at the door and Nakeya is kissing Kaden.

Feel like having some visitors Juan says peeking through the door?

Sure, we welcome all visitors especially if they have food?

How are you feeling kiddo Roman says as he looks at his new grandson?"

Sore, very sore Nakeya says nothing like when i had Gabriella.

Do you need anything going down to the cafeteria to see what they have?"

Some ice please babe a cup of crushed ice and some cranberry juice.

I'll be right back to anyone else what something, i come with you.

He is so long he's going to be tall Rosetta says as she holds Kaden.

Handsome little dude Allison says as she waits her turn to hold Kaden.

Here you go Nakeya and get you an extra-large cup of crushed ice .

Thanks babe you know how i love eating that crushed ice.

You finally got your little man Roman says to Rafael smiling.

Let the spoiling begin Rafael says this is one of my best days

Dr. Onye comes in to tell Nakeya she will be ready to leave in a couple of days?

It's not like last time I'll take off for a couple of weeks to nurse you back to health. Rafael tells Nakeya.

Working from home for a couple of weeks, are we Mr. Romas?

Hey James, yeah to help Nakeya after the birth of our son Kaden?

Congratulations on the little one saw the pictures very handsome.

Thanks, James, for helping me and Carlos during this time.

I will handle everything else at home. Feel free to call, don't you worry James say we got your back.

Let's go home Kaden so you and mommy can get some rest.

Oh, give me my godson can't wait to hold him?

Kaden Ivan Romas welcome to the world. Hey, was that a smile?

That was not a smile, it was a sign of him having gas.

Shut up Rafael, Maria says he loves his aunties don't you Kaden?

How are you feeling Nakeya, Rafael asked as she sat on the couch?

"Very sore maybe I should go lay down upstairs in the room a bit.

I'll help you Nakeya, Rafael says then the rest of the family leave.

Thanks, you guys' Nakeya says as she slowly walks up the steps.

I'll bring dinner in a little bit. Let me help you get your pajamas on?

Okay, dinner was great, thanks for all your help. You just rest nite.

There you want to see your baby brother Gabriella. That's your little brother Kaden. You're still Daddy's little girl don't you worry. Look at that smile.

Oh, hey Dad, you want the TV left on or you want it turned off?

Sure, turn it off your mom is already sleep how is Nakeya feeling?

You okay my love looks like you're in pain need some medicine?

Yeah, please I will be fine in no time just hold me babe.

I can do that now, take the medicine and I will hold you honey.

Hey none of that or we will be having baby number three.

No, I have my daughter and son we're good for now maybe later?

When did you knock down the wall? It looks great more room.

Me, Juan, and Jose did it when you were in the hospital.

That's why you were late picking us up widening the nursery area.

76

Maybe we should get a bigger house and give my parents this house? We can find another house for our growing family.

But can we afford it now, Rafael, with the new baby and our wedding?

Maybe we should wait till I get back into the working field?

Stop worrying Nakeya things will work out besides business is up.

Rafael we just had a baby, got engaged, plus our wedding in a month?

"Stop, stop worrying Nakeya our wedding will be amazing don't.

Sorry Rafael, just don't want you to be overwhelmed about anything?

Before you left work i thought it was great to start saving for a nest egg.

Business is going well and now Na'keya get some sleep please?

Okay we're both tired and you know what i really love you?

Love you Mrs. Romas forever and always in my heart.

Mrs. Romas has a nice ring to it, doesn't it, though Rafael says.

Yes, it does Nakeya says agreeing with him then kisses him nite.

Kaden hey baby boy? How's mommy's baby boy? Gabriella what are you doing baby girl? Rafael baby, can you hear me, Rafael huh

Can you help me please come into the nursery for a minute?

What are you doing Nakeya here let me do this you sit here?

It's too soon for you to me trying to move around Nakeya.

Please allow me to help you with the kids, that's why I'm here.

But I can do some things Rafael, I'm not a handicapped babe.

Weeks passed by and Rafael came into the house yelling Nakeya, Nakeya.

Um yeah, the kids are sleeping and I'm getting some work done.

Sorry how it feels to be back to work Rafael says peeping in?

Great, I'm going to shower you have company hello Allison.

You mean he allowed you to go back to work Allison says?

He didn't allow me to do anything, he supported my choice.

If you say so Allison says, Nakeya looked at her slightly irritated.

Anyway, Nakeya says what do you want? The following day Nakeya gets a surprise when feeding the kids.

Where is that sexy thing of yours at Nakeya asked Mona?

If you're talking about my fiancé, he is on his way home which is none of your business.

Hey Mrs. Romas, nice to see you. Hello Mona Rosetta says meanly.

Just wanted to come by and see the family and be nice.

Na'keya baby where you at then stops as he sees Mona? Hey there sexy Mona replies, Nakeya looked at her let's say if looks could kill.

Don't you have somewhere to be, Maria says coming in the door?

As a matter of fact, I do Mona replied to Maria with a half smirk.

See you around sexy Mona says as she walks out the front door.

Ooh I hate that girl Nakeya says to Maria she's a pain in my butt?

She does that because she knows you get mad Rafael says.

I got a bad feeling about her she's trouble Nakeya says no good.

How was work Rafael tell me all about your day, anything new?

You hungry babe, can warm your dinner back up as you shower?

Rafael whispers in my ear "I'm hungry but not for food he laughs.

Ha,ha real funny nasty man maybe later i can help you out ?

Where are my babies Daddy wants to kiss his Prince and Princess?

Both are asleep Nakeya says but you can kiss their beautiful mom?

Oh, Nakeya, how was your first day back at work tell me?

Good my first day was great, oh honey flowers for me ah baby?

Yes, a present for your first day back to work and make you smile.

I think I love you Rafael, I really think that I love you, Rafael.

You think Nakeya really you hear that mom she thinks not know?

Why did Jose hire Mona, Nakeya asked Rafael. How did you know?
Rafael, that trick will be in there with a short skirt. Nakeya is not
nice. Can she even count Maria replies, Nakeya laughed?

Run Jose they got their claws out Rafael says. Jose, why her?

Why did you hire that girl Nakeya asked? She's trouble with a
capital T Maria replied.

She needed a job besides she qualified for that position.

I'm surprised she can fill out an application, Maria lets go.

What's on your mind Nakeya you been quiet since they left?

Nakeya nothing honeys just thinking about some stuff.

Do you like girls like Mona and Rafael? Nakeya blurts out. Huh?

You have nothing to worry about. I love my family too much to
have someone come in and ruin a good thing."

It has been a long time."

Yeah i can tell so does my back but did you have to Nakeya?

You scratched my back like a wild woman Nakeya.

Sorry but when you hit my spots you know what it does to me.

I have you down for eleven on Monday sorry Tuesday.

Yes, we're still on 653 Red Gull Street, Mona tells a customer.

May I come in Jose says to Rafael watching Mona answering calls?

Okay, see you then Ms. Hubbet, Bye. What's going on, Mona says?

I'm getting swamped out here, no wonder you need a secretary.

Hold that thought Mona says, I got you down see you then. Have a good evening.

Girl, please tell me why was Mona in business and not at the desk?

Huh, Nakeya says start over. I'm pissed, Maria says. Before I got here went to the shop to pick up the kids and Mona was sitting at the desk. Me and Jose got into a little disagreement, and she put her two cents in. I told her to shut up and she rolled her eyes. She is going to cause trouble, Nakeya replied.

Meanwhile back at the shop, Mona speaks to Rafael.

Hey Mona, he replied while walking back to his office.

Oh, I love how you say my name Rafael, he shakes his head.

"Where is my brother Jose asked as he came in the front door?

In the back going to his office, Mona replied licking her lips.

I can do it myself Rafael says to Mona as she follows him. Thank you.

Sure thing, sweet cheeks do you need any assistance, Rafael?

Um, Jose glad your back please come to my office let's talk?

Yeah bro what's on your mind, I know what's on her mind?

Jose, Mona is going to cause so much trouble and you know why?

Never mind her, she does a good job then Jose glances out the window.

Is that Na'keya walking up the walkway and, who else oh no?

Why do you feel you need to be in my business, Mona says to Maria?

What's going on up here Jose and Rafael come up as they hear yelling?

Maria says, I was kindly telling Mona to stay out of our business.

Right, Jose says. Mona, you can leave now, see you tomorrow.

Goodbye everyone, then she smiled at Rafael as she left.

Maria calls her a tramp as she sees her looking in the window.

That's not nice, don't laugh Nakeya she loves an audience.

No replied Maria it's not nice, but it's so true, Nakeya replied.

Rafael and Jose, Maria said watch out for that trick? Rafael leaves and sees that Mona is still outside. Nakeya goes outside to calm Rafael down when Mona sees her and pretends that they kissed, and it worked. What the hell, Nakeya says oh hell no?

Nakeya, Nakeya wait let me explain? Maria looks out what the hell?

I saw her lips on your lips Rafael you're caught don't deny it.

She tried kissing me and I backed up Rafael tries to explain?

"Didn't look that way, Nakeya said. You need me to whip on that?"

Stop it Maria, Jose that's my girl and if she needs me to tap that ass.

Sorry Nakeya, told you she's trouble Rafael? Don't touch me?

He will tell you, tell me what Mona tell me what bitch?

Tell her what Mona there is nothing to tell nothing happened?

That you touched me of course Rafael no matter where i am?

What, Mona you know damn well I never touched you?

81

Mona you better stop lying on me that never happened and you know it.

I resign Mona says, I'll have my lawyer contact you, Rafael.

What lawyer I never touched you. You're fired Mona, Jose said.

Rafael, you kiss Mona, no Maria honest no time have i ever?

She set me up and she told Nakeya we kissed. Nakeya, I love you?

How could you Rafael do you not love me or find me attractive?

Nakeya, I love you, our family, and our kid's life. I never kissed Mona she's talking about harassment charges.

My business, my world and my family will be turned upside down?

Later that evening Enrique pays a visit to Mona at her condo.

Enrique, what do I owe this pleasure to? What happened today?

Start talking Mona, Enrique says, and he doesn't look happy?

About what Mona don't play me for a fool, start talking?

You know why you are lying on my brother, Mona?

If he comes back to me, I'll drop the charges? He loves Nakeya not you.

Don't destroy his happy home, Enrique says as he opens the door?

Should it have been me not Nakeya, our kids and our wedding?

Back at the house Nakeya and Rafael continue to argue then Nakeya says?

Rafael the wedding, No Nakeya don't say it please. The wedding is off."

Honey. Keya i only love you sorry Nakeya, should have listened.

I already fed the kids, gave them their baths. Daddy where is mommy;

Rafael tells Gabbie she's resting? I hate Mona for making my life a living hell, Nakeya says crying to herself in the room.

Maria and Allison decide to give Mona a piece of their mind.

Rafael will be mine; Mona tells someone on the phone then a knock.

She better not be talking to him, Allison says as she say the phone?

I'll call you back, Mona says to the girl on the phone then hangs up.

"What do you two want, Mona asked as she smirks at Allison?

Mona my brother never touched you, I know he's not like that.

So, what if he didn't, Mona says what's it to you or her anyway?

Why are you doing this to him, Mona, you used to love him? Huh?

The life Nakeya has should have been mine, Mona replied. Our house, our kids, this should be our wedding.

Girl, you need therapy, Allison says, still trying to understand what Maria said.

Tell Nakeya the truth about nothing happening between you two?

Why would I do that Maria, tell Nakeya that nothing happened?

It's the right thing to do, Allison and Maria both said.

If I don't then what Maria? Maria slowly walks toward Mona, she steps back.

You don't want to know; Mona replies to Maria do you want to find out?

Is that a threat Maria, you just threaten me you know who i am?

Mona, do you remember who I am replies to Maria then smiles.

Oh, Mona it's gonna be trouble if you don't Allison added.

Get out of my house both of you, Mona says a bit shaken.

Think about it, Maria says, yeah sure Mona says then slams the door.

Maria and Allison pay a visit to Nakeya. Girl you, okay?

I love him so much Allison. How is he gonna do this to me, our family? I trusted him."

You really think Rafael kissed her, really?

I saw them kissing.

Or did you see what she wanted you to see?

Maria, I'm not following. We should tell you about Mona and Rafael's past."

Their past?

We're gonna tell Nakeya your past with Mona.

Then she will know what we are dealing with.

Mona has known us for years. Anyway, Rafael and Mona went out a couple of times. One day, she wanted him to meet her at her house.

I don't want to hear anymore, stop.

Listen.

When he got there, he walked in and saw Mona entertaining the local pharmacist. As he was leaving some guys approached him. Words were said later that night, something went down, and was identified as the suspect?

What happened Maria, Rafael, someone tell me?

I supposedly beat up Mona and broke her arm. Well long story short, Rosetta says we feared for our son's life. We sent him to Argentina to stay with family, he was only seventeen. And yesterday when I saw her had to leave the room brought up bad memories.

You could have told me Rafael? I'm speechless me to he said.

That's why when we met, I had grown up in Argentina and that explains why you remember Maria, Jose, and Juan not me. Was already gone when you guys were in school.

Rafael baby, I'm so very sorry I didn't believe you?

I should have told you. Now that you know, how do we get her to tell the truth?

There is a knock at the door.

Mr. Rafael Romas please sign here.

What's this?

"You've been served. Good evening."

This has gone too far. Mom, Dad, where are you going? We'll be back in a few.

"Where are you going Juan asked but they just left?

A few hours later they returned but they were not alone.

I want you to meet my best friend and, Mona's mom Rosalie.

Nice to meet you, Nakeya says as she turns around to see Rafael.

Rafael gets a hold of Mona we have a plan that might work.

Rafael tells Mona that you have changed your mind? Why will that work?

My future with Nakeya our family is at stake, Rafael says.

I'm sorry my daughter is causing you and your family pain. You are my dearest friend."

"It's not your fault Rosalie your daughter is grown.

Hello Mona, your mom's over here, Rafael says then begins to say because I changed my mind about us of course, almost choking?

Can you come over so we can talk and clear the air?

Do I love you, sure never stopped seeing you in a few, bye.

That sick bitch, Nakeya says. She'll be here in half an hour.

Maria and Jose can you, Rosetta tells them something then they leave.

Nakeya you don't have to be here, Rosetta says hugging her.

Stay you're not in the way, Rafael says and kisses her on the lips.

My daughters are in love with you and, she will drop the charges.

Let's hope Nakeya says around the corner, then silence then.

There is a knock at the side door, it's Mona smiling.

Hey there lover boy you finally came to your senses.

You can say that.

Where should I put my bags?

Your bags oh of course In our room.

Wait a minute Mona, let's talk about getting the air clear?

I never meant to hurt you Rafael, just got jealous of seeing you with her.

Promise to drop the false charges to get rid of Nakeya?

Why Mona, you left me no choice Rafael, but you left her so were good.

Mommy hey, did you hear we're back together this time no drama.

Mona, what you did was wrong baby.

You do anything for love, right Rafael tell her?

Ms. Hernandez, you're under arrest for filing a false report.

You set me up Rafael, you lied to me my love?

Anything for love then Rafael hugs Nakeya as they handcuffed her.

Nakeya you stole him from me, Mona says as she sees them kiss.

Thank you, gentlemen. I'm glad that's over, Nakeya sees Mona crying in the cop car as it drives away.

Now to plan our wedding Nakeya, because i can't wait to make you, my wife?

I love you so much.

Let's go suit shopping gentlemen, going to marry the love of my life.

Maria, Allison and Nakeya have to go get refitted for the dresses.

Ms. Williams welcome back. Thank you, Ms. Rich Congratulations, on your son.

Ladies put your dresses on then come out. Well Maria we have to loosen here and tighten here. Next Nakeya some tighten up there and loosen a hair or two down here? Oh, my Allison, what we have to tighten here, add some more fabric in the stomach area here.

Allison, you put on some pounds here lately you sure you're not.

I'm late Allison says then changes Maria and Nakeya look at each other.

Girl you preg—

Don't say it.

Would it be so bad?

I just got my raise at work which means more work hours.

You're selfish, Maria says as she pays for the alterations.

I just want some time with Enrique before sharing my time with a baby.

Mom would love it she's going to flip when she hears the news.

Don't tell Enrique.

I want to see if I am.

Pregnant Allison the word is pregnant you can say it, Maria says.

All right ladies, I'll work on these alterations. Final fitting next Friday before the big day.

Oh, the party is tomorrow evening at Yes, starting at eight. See ya then. Bye, girl," Nakeya said, hanging up the phone.

I got this bad ass outfit to show you Maria says to Nakeya.

I have nothing new to wear Rosetta says in return.

This is an outfit to wear for a baby shower not club Na'keya replied.

Not feeling that color but nice outfit Lydia said to Rosetta.

Girl let's just go shopping Allison said to Nakeya

Let me grab my purse girl Nakeya told Allison, Maria follows.

So, did you think any more about my offer to come work for me? A family business, Nakeya asked Maria?

Yes, maybe in the first of the year I'll work in your office?

What size am I since having the babies losing then gaining not sure Nakeya asks herself?

Try this dress on Nakeya, Maria passed to her.

What let me see Allison said to Nakeya?

What's wrong with that Rosetta asked Nakeya?

Love the skirt but, then Nakeya stops and turns around to show.

But what does the shirt look it's really tight around my chest?

Grab Nakeya a bigger size for her breast to breathe, Maria says. Nakeya asked Allison to pass her a bigger size she was closer.

I'm buying this outfit; Nakeya says now shoes. Nakeya, which ones you want then Lydia points and waits for a reaction from Nakeya. Get the black ones next to the gold ones, Nakeya replied to Maria.

"Thank you, come again the sales lady says to Nakeya as they leave.

Now to get our hair and nails done, Maria says to the girls.

Allison is running a few minutes later she sneaked out as Nakeya was trying on different pairs of shoes.

Rosetta, you come sit here and get started Maria you seat next to your mom relied on Nakeya looking at the door?

Allison, you're back Nakeya says sorry I'm late had to go somewhere.

Me, Nakeya says you sit here, and you sit here the nail lady told Allison.

Would any of you ladies like a glass of wine while getting serviced?

Oh yes please the ladies say except Allison. Thanks for asking.

None for me, Allison says do you have any juice put it on the rocks?

Allison, have you gone to the doctors, yet Rosetta asked?

No, but got an appointment with Dr. Onye for tomorrow at 9 am?

Oh yeah Nakeya says you will like her she's nice. "Your nails look great Na'keya replied to Allison.

We have two hours before it starts replied to Nakeya to Lydia.

Where are the guys going, Nakeya asked Lydia?

Some clubs on Welsh and Green Court not sure of the name. Lydia replied to Nakeya you mean Pleasure Palace Gentlemen's Club nice.

Lydia said they were like schoolboys before she left. All the girls are meeting over here. You got the address? 765 Jokane Drive it's the brick house, see you when you get here. Lydia was saying while hanging up the phone.

Girl don't mess up your make-up. I'm don't not forget to put yours on Nakeya replied to Allison's smart remark.

Girls just think in a couple hours I will be Mrs. Rafael Juan Romas. All jokes aside, I'm glad things worked out Maria says to Nakeya.

"Ah Maria don't make me cry? A toast to my future sister-in-law. May you and my brother continue to have happiness throughout the rest of your lives.

Cheers, cheers ok girls time to party let's paint the night red. We get to the front door, and we're greeted with a male stipper dressed as a cowboy he then says welcome to the Aura G-Spot.

Allison and Maria what have you done still smiling? Oh my God Nakeya says to Maria, are you blushing Nakeya?

"Which one of you ladies is getting married the male stripper asked?

Lydia and Maria pointed at Nakeya; my name is Valentino follow me.

Wish it was me Na'keya's friend Carmen says smiling at Valentino.

Oh my God Nakeya put the money in his G-string someone yells out. Look at those abs, Lydia says to Maria. That's what we call a caliente especial [hot special] Rosetta says touching his chest.

Dude she is beautiful Enrique says to Juan easy young man.

Who's the lucky man the female stripper dressed as a cheerleader asked?

That would be me Rafael replied to the stripper, I'm Blazing Cinnamon follow me gentlemen.

Go Ralphie, go Ralphie. Put it in her thong Juan shouted to Rafael?

Shake it, shake it Roman yells then she sits on his lap oh my God Roman says.

The girl was glad were not driving. I'm so drunk Nakeya told Maria in a drunken voice.

You get some rest and you're getting married in seven hours. See you then Maria replies to Na'keya laughing at her talking drunk.

Our wedding day Nakeya says happily. Oh no Rafael don't touch me like that? Ah that feels so good. I love you mi amor [my love]. Nakeya and Rafael are in their room fooling around, Maria says.

Hey, it's bad luck to see the bride", Maria jokingly told Rafael as he was leaving.

Don't be so old-fashioned Rafael replied to Maria, running out the door.

Knock, knock may we come in? You made a beautiful bride pumpkin, thank you Daddy.

Where's Mom right here you're so Beautiful Nakeya.

Mommy don't cry your mess up your make-up.

You're just so beautiful Nakeya and we are so excited and proud.

Who has Kaden and Gabriella? I want to say it's Vivian, yeah her.

Vivian from the office Nakeya replied getting touched up.

Doesn't Kaden look very handsome? Gabriella looks so sweet. My grandbabies are getting so big. Thanks for the pictures, they're precious.

You're welcome, Nakeya gave her mom pictures of her grandkids.

Almost ready to walk down there to meet your future husband?

Who gives this woman to wed this man?

We do Nakeya's parents reply to the priest's question.

Nakeya do you take this man to be your husband?

Yes, I do Nakeya replied.

Rafael, do you take this woman to be your wife?

Yes, I do, Rafael replied.

Forsaken all others Rafael, yes, I do? Nakeya will you do the same?

Yes, I do with all my heart always to love and honor each other.

Please place the ring on his finger. Now you place the ring on her finger. Repeat after me: I Rafael now, you repeat after me. I Nakeya. In the power vested in me now pronounce you Husband and Wife you may kiss your bride. The priest announces to all the wedding party now introducing Mr. and Mrs. Rafael Juan Romas. The wedding planner announces as they walk into the reception.

Ah look at my baby, Nakeya's parents say as they walk down the aisle.

Wow look at this place Rafael it's amazing Nakeya says.

Glad you like it Rafael says designed just for you on our special day. Nakeya talking to Rafael and thanking him for the beautiful day.

Everyone's enjoying our wedding day, Nakeya says to Rafael.

The first dance Mr. and Mrs. Romas the wedding planner says to the bride and groom.

That's my song oh, wobble baby, wobble baby. Nakeya and the wedding party are all dancing enjoying both slow and fast songs.

All the single ladies please stand, Nakeya says. Mrs. Romas throws the flowers one of the guests yells jokingly.

Ready on three 1,2,3, then she threw it into the crowd of ladies.

Oh my God, I really caught it Allison says to herself in a shocked voice.

Gentlemen gather around Rafael and he's about to throw the garter.

Mr. Romas just the garter belt Nakeya tells Rafael laughing.

Ralphie, my boy Roman yells this way pointing to Enrique secretly.

Throw it this way another guy yells. Ready on three 1,2,3. Enrique catches it and smiles at Allison.

Your attention please as best man, a toast to Congratulate him on his marriage. May he and NaKeya remain happy as they grow old together. Te amo[love you] Rafael. Te amo usted[I love you] Jose. Rafael, my brother, a toast to you two. May you always be happy as you journey the road of marriage. At times, the road may be rough, but it will smooth out again. Welcome to the family. Love you two. Juan is giving a heartfelt toast to his brother and new sister-in-law, and he cries.

Well, you guys continue to party Rafael says. My wife and I have to catch a plane to go on our honeymoon. Love all you guys. Thank you all for coming to share our very special day. Nakeya and Rafael tell their wedding guest while heading to the door.

Bye Gabriella, bye Kaden mommy and daddy will see you in a couple of days love you both.

They will be fine Maria says as they give Nakeya and Rafael hugs.

Thanks again.

our pleasure bro. We are godparents. Enjoy your honeymoon.

Oh, don't you worry about that Rafael says we will smiling.

Call you tomorrow, Nakeya tells Maria. You'll be busy. All the bags are in the truck and the tickets are in the front pocket Juan tells Rafael.

Oh, I see them Nakeya says to Rafael thanks for all your help.

Rafael thanks Juan for his help getting things in order.

Hope I got everything, Nakeya says looking out the window.

We can get it there Nakeya they have stores Rafael replies.

Ready Mrs. Romas yes Mr. Romas let's go on our honeymoon?

That song we danced to for our first dance was beautiful.

Makes me think of us even though it's in Spanish still got goosebumps.

Can I get your luggage sir and, how long will your car be here, the airport attendant asked Rafael.

Just until morning made arrangements for it to be picked up.

The name of the other party? You're all set to enjoy your flight.

Thank you, Rafael says back.

Nakeya are you nervous, but baby how come?

It feels like the first time we got together I be alright.

You will forget all about your nerves when you get some drinks.

Now boarding Flight 509 to Virgin Islands and Saint Thomas.

That's us Rafael tells Nakeya, you got everything?

Let's go, Rafael says to Nakeya our honeymoon awaits.

Hello, your tickets please. Congratulations on your wedding. Go straight and then turn left when you pass the double doors.

"This plane is huge Nakeya tells Rafael, I'm so excited right now.

Planes about to take off in two minutes find your seats buckle up.

Good evening, care for a drink or perhaps a snack the stewardess asked?

Nakeya says she will take a white wine and for you sir.

Corona with lime and can you get use some nachos with cheese.

Back in a few the flight attendant asked Nakeya and Rafael in first class.

"You're beautiful Nakeya and you're sweet Rafael that is why I love you. I think I'll marry you wait a minute as I just did.

Ha ha very funny Nakeya, Rafael replies and continues talking while in flight.

We will reach our destination in two minutes please remain seated the pilot said over the loudspeaker.

You enjoy the movie babe, sure which part i saw was busy talking to my wife?

Thank you for flying nationwide. Watch your step. Thank you for coming again. Let's find our luggage and go to our villa. I grabbed our bags. Mr. and Mrs. Romas, I am Jerry, your driver follows me.

Oh, my really a limo Rafael. It's our day anything for my queen. The airport attendant helps load their bags into the limo.

Thirteen miles away ooh babe it has a sunroof look at all the stores. It's so pretty here Nakeya says. Oh, Rafael you really out did yourself. Wanted to make our wedding day special Rafael replied. My name is Max, your greeter Mr. and Mrs. Romas your villa right this way.

Nakeya says to Rafael while still talking to each other in the room. Oh my God it's perfect. Your keys, thanks, don't pick me up. Wow looks at those tall trees they look like towers. Take a look around i'll put our stuff away. The room is so pretty, there's plenty of food and it's a pool located on the patio. Perhaps for a late-night swim. You realize it's one thirty in the morning Rafael. I'll go change, so what do you think like what you see? Yes, I do, would you like a drink Nakeya?

The kids are good. You called Nakeya yes to say good night. Na'keya and Rafael begin to talk to each other again and reply to each other a good bit. Sorry no problema senora [lady no problem]. That feels so good. Ah that feels so amazing. I like it when you suck on my nipples like that. I'm getting so hard you gonna make me cum Nakeya. Love to hear you moan Nakeya. AH you gato[cat] you scratched my back up. Sorry you just feel so good, can't help it. Good morning Mrs.Romas, morning dear. Ready for breakfast. I'm starving? Excuse me, Mr. and Mrs. Romas. I'm Maureen your housekeeper throughout your stay. Nice to meet you. Breakfast is served out on the patio. We have assorted juices, assorted waters, assorted wines with some French toast, sausages, and assorted fruits. Anything else before I leave? NO, we're all set. See you at lunch time enjoy your day. Everything looks good, eat up we have a busy day. How should I dress Rafael? Sexy Oh you grab the camera Nakeya? Let's go. How much does this all-cost babes? Why is Nakeya our honeymoon my gift to you? Just curious about five thousand? What can't we afford that? Stop it Nakeya. We can get a few high paying contracting jobs, a couple of bonuses even. Thinking about expanding to another place. AH honey that is great. Look at that water, it's so blue and crystal clear. Maria is thinking about coming to work at my firm. When in the beginning of the year. Business is very good for a couple of clients. They referred me to some other clients that led to more business. I'm proud of you babe. We're sitting on the pink sandy beach. Nakeya and Rafael are still talking to each other and replying to each other. The sky is so blue like it was painted. This other beach's sand so white it looks like snow. Snap some pictures of this and that. Then stares in amazement of all the attractions. The first couple of days we spent in Saint Thomas. While we were there, we visited the Coki Beach famous for kayaking, white sandy beaches, and nature trails. We walked the trails holding hands. Saw all kinds of birds, different wildlife we snapped so many pictures of Rafael. He also snapped some of me.

When we went to Magens Bay. We came across the Coral World Ocean Park. This place has both an indoor and outdoor aquarium. Rafael snapped a quick picture of me holding a starfish. Great picture of him swimming with the turtles. Hey look, a seal is behind you. Look at the baby sharks. Tonight, we'll go and explore the nightlife. We danced, drank and took pictures. Just had a ball listening to the different drums, salsa, and reggae. You can't help but get lost inside the beat. The drum sounds like a heartbeat. While visiting Saint Croix we went on a tour Where they make the famous Cruzan rum. Took some Pictures of their distillery, sampled different flavors of the rum. Main Street Plaza was next on our list. Two hours later, we must have visited each store in this plaza. The best for bargain shopping, Nakeya says. You think you got enough bags Rafael says as he carries them? Look what I snapped honey? A picture of me with sauce on my face. Look at that view Rafael, it's breathtaking. We got so many pictures. I'm going to hate leaving. I can't wait to show these pictures to everybody. You ready our flight leaves in ten minutes. Flight 509 is now boarding. That's us honey next stop Home sweet Home.

Thank you for flying Transamerica please watch your step.

Nakeya, yeah babe wonder if? Yes, Jose remembered to bring the truck back here for us. These are all the bags; Nakeya replies I hope so.

Next stop 765 Johane Drive. There here someone says, Roman there back.

Jose asked Nakeya and Rafael about their honeymoon. It was so Beautiful, Nakeya says.

Gabriella and Kaden, Mommy and Daddy have missed their babies.

Nakeya asked Maria how they were. They were fine, no problems.

Nakeya asked the family to gather around closer. Come look at the pictures we took. That is a beautiful place, Lydia says. That is where we stayed, Amazing Lydia said still looking.

Lydia says out loud the water looks so blue. I'm jealous Rosetta says.

Maria says look at that dress and those shoes are a great choice. I have to borrow that. If it fits you, Nakeya replied.

Enrique asked Rafael if they checked out any sites. Yeah, the Coral World Aquarium was pretty cool.

Rafael says we had fun but so glad to be back. Now back to reality.

Nakeya talks to Rafael while getting ready for bed. Back to work, Nakeya says while checking her messages. We have an interview for a new associate.

Get some sleep work in the morning. Mi amor [my love] have a good day. ADIOS. [bye]

Hey sis, welcome back, we got you a basket of fruit and coffee to enjoy.

Nakeya, Mr. Karim Keymon is waiting in your office. Thank you, Liz, for telling my sister I will be in her office when I'm done.

Mr. Keymon Good morning I'm Mrs. Nakeya Romas nice to meet you. So, tell me about yourself, Mr. Keymon.

Karim replied in my country mostly office but attended school in the states to become a Law Assistant.

Nakeya then asked Karim how long have you been practicing law?

Karim replies for almost three years. If hired, when can you start?

Nakeya continues to ask Karim some questions and he is replying back to Nakeya starts looking over his resume. Your resume is very impressive, i see you know Professor Nelson. Yes, he told me to *apply.*

Nakeya then asked Mr. Karim this question? How old are you, Mr. Keymon?

Karim replies I'm twenty-four but in two days twenty-five. Will be in touch she then silences.

Nakeya asked Karim if he had any questions for me?

Karim replies to Nakeya actually yes is there anything that is stopping you from hiring me right now you said my resume was impressive, plus a letter of recommendation. From your college Professor Martin Nelson.

Sorry to intrude but i like his attitude, spunkiness he's like a male you? Excuse us Mr. Keymon as I am talking with my partner? Maria, what do you think? We need someone of his talent besides Professor Nelson who recommended him and, you know, he does not recommend anyone.

Nakeya asked Karim to come back to Mr. Keymon, we decided.

Karim replies back to Nakeya please you can call me Karim.

Nakeya replies alright then Karim when can you start?

Tomorrow at eight sounds great, we will see you then.

Maria says to Karim "Keep that same edge you'll go far.

Nakeya shakes Karim's hands as she welcomes him aboard.

Karim replies Thank you so very much both of you much Thanks.

We should give him the Boone case to see how he's in the courtroom.

Rafael says you're home early must have been a good day.

Nakeya replied yeah, we just hired someone. The interviewer?

Nakeya replied to back good news travels fast. Heard he's spunky a male version of you.

Nakeya replied back he does remind me of myself when I first started.

Dinner then straight to bed need to get some rest feeling tired. Getting an early start Karim? Good morning, Nakeya, I am indeed.

Came here to read over the case that you gave me to see what i'm facing?

When we go to court in a few days want to be ready for anything. This little space right here is your office for the time being, but it will look like ours with your own private bathroom, any questions?

Vivian says, well he just jumped right on in feet first. Mr. Boone will be here in a few minutes, where should I take him Mrs. Romas?

Nakeya replies in Karim's office that the two should get to know each other. Mr. Boone, Good morning, could you please follow me.

Nakeya introduced Karim to Mr. Boone, and they replied to each other. Meet our new associate Mr. Karim Keymon. He will be taking over your case.

Karim is talking to Mr. Boone about his case in his office. While he was reading over his case, he found something which might entitle him to more money, like twenty-eight percent of the company's assets. Really correct me if I'm wrong but didn't you help start and co-create this business? Also bring in some of your personal clients that followed you.

Nakeya says aloud to herself can't believe I missed that?

Maria says I'm feeling a lot better, Mr. Karim about court. Karim replies to Maria thank you for what? Trusting me alone with this. Karim replies to Liz welcome aboard Mr. Karim. Thank you, Liz.

Karim is talking to Nakeya about going into court. Mrs. Romas, good day. Willy, how are you? No hard feelings today when I win.

Court starts in five minutes.

Allison says Sorry I'm late you only missed Willy and he don't count.

Maria replies to your right on time to see Willy eat some crow.

Karim asked his client Mr. Boone, was he ready for court?

Karim tells the ladies to go in first and holds the door for them. Karim says to Mr. Boone please state your full name for the court.

Mr. Boone swallows then reply my name is Stuart Glen Boone.

Karim then asked Mr. Boone, and where did you work, Sir?

Mr. Boone replies to Jackson Mutual and worked there for forty years.

Karim asked Mr. Boone and you helped create this particular office. I object to your Honor. Overruled. Is it safe to say, Mr. Boone, that you also brought in your share of new clients to this office over time?

Mr. Boone replies, "of course I did a lot of them very much so.

Willy yells Objection your Honor he's leading the witness.

Judge replied. Overruled. What? Please continue, Mr. Keymon.

Mr. Boone then replied, I brought in several clients personally from my other job that closed down, which in return brought me more clients.

Karim replied with so you were getting clients as well as providing clients?

The judge says we established that Mr. Keymon, what angle you trying to make Mr. Keymon.

Karim replies to your Honor Mr. Boone is entitled to more money twenty-eight percent to be exact. According to the assets from the buyout. Look at this form if you read the highlighted section, it explains he is entitled to more? Courts in recess stay for two hours.

The Judge comes back after reviewing the contract Mr. Boone you are entitled to more. Ninety percent more than you have proved to me that you did more than your fair share. The rule is for the Plaintiff for Twenty-eight thousand dollars in back rearrange. Starting tomorrow you will be issued a check until the end of Life. Three thousand a month for pain and suffering. Case is dismissed.

Mr. Boone turns to Karim and Thanks him for all his help.

Mr. Boone then turns to Nakeya and Maria thank you.

Maria tells Karim not bad for the first case Win. Willy passed us by saying I'm impressed then leaves. We should celebrate on your first Win.

Nakeya tells Karim that he's going to enjoy having dinner on us.

Liz starts making reservations for Nakeya. Good evening, do you have a reservation? A few minutes from a call table for Mrs. Romas and associates please follow me to your table.

Liz Congratulates Karim on his first Win then she hangs up.

Maria begins to introduce Karim to the husbands. Nakeya begins to toast to our newest addition and Man of the hour Karim Keymon. Maria suddenly says you should have a name. Nakeya replies what if we call him Scorpion?" Think about it, he just goes for the obvious and no questions asked?

Well, hey Allison glad you could make it Enrique stepped out? Something's wrong with Allison look, Nakeya said to Maria?

Allison asked Nakeya and Maria if they could talk looking teary eyed? I have to speak with you privately. Sure. Excuses us guys, they kept on talking.

Allison begins talking but shaking at the same time then says i'm well you know? Please don't make me say it, Maria? Knocked up, preggos, with child pick one.

Nakeya hugs Allison. How did Enrique take the news? He doesn't know yet just came straight here. Allison replies back, Enrique doesn't even know I had a Dr's appointment, what am I going to do, how will he take the news, Allison says as she's talking to herself? He stepped out, Nakeya said. You want me to tell him?

Rafael walks over to us and asks Nakeya what's going on? What's all the screaming and whispering about?

Nakeya replies to Rafael, guess what Allison is pregnant? I knew it when Enrique would get sick or just started getting tired, Congratulations.

Allison says to Nakeya maybe we should talk at home. Rafael replies to Allison telling him here with family he will be so Excited.

Maria says out loud must say Enrique and Allison make a cute, odd couple, never would have guessed them talking or liking each other. Rafael asked Nakeya if they had begun planning for the wedding. Nakeya replies No not yet, why have you? Yes, we have really Rafael, Nakeya says looking surprised. The day at the office

Excuse me Mr. Keymon, Maria says. We would like to discuss a plan or strategy with Mr. Clergets case, so we decided to give it to you?

Karim agrees to take the case on since he won the last case but said he had a conference call, and they could discuss afterwards. Karim starts reading over the case and begins taking notes about his client's case. Karim talks to Maria and Nakeya he begins by saying Mr. Cleggets has a living will but, the beneficiary is not his current wife but his mistress of several years. Karim says jokingly busy man. Don't know how to go around that to tell something without breach of contract, Karim starts talking to himself as Maria and Nakeya watch?

Discussing his will with his current wife but, another woman. Karim then leaves without saying a word. Couple of hours later Karim comes back into the office smiling.

Maria jokingly says someone's in a much happier place.

Karim proceeds to say guess who just won another case?

Nakeya and Maria look at each other, Karim what are you talking about? Well had to call for an emergency Will reading, and some things came out, but we did not in any way breach his contract. Well way to go Mr. Scorpion Nakeya says. Go ahead with your bad self.

Karim replies Yeah guess I am like a Scorpion cause my wins are leaving the competition dazed. Then he laughs as he leaves.

Nakeya just shakes her head, he's so crazy talking to herself.

Maria says Karim sure is making a name for himself, don't you think?

He would make a good 2nd partner one day. Anything is possible.

Maria says he looks up to you Nakeya and he wants your approval. Nakeya replied to you really think so, i had not noticed, Wow. Maria replied to girl, "the only thing he doesn't do is drool? Whenever you come into the room his whole face lights up, Maria, I think you're exaggerating? Karim has a crush on you. Better watch out girl.

Oh, shut up Maria let's go we have an appointment at the Bridal shop.

Maria whispers to Nakeya, "can't believe Allison can't find anything to wear? Allison says to herself try that dress on of course you won't look like a whale. Nakeya tells Allison you're not even showing why you are tripping? Allison replies I gained three pounds there goes my figure.

Maria and Nakeya looked at each other then they busted out laughing.

Allison continues talking to Maria and Nakeya while looking at dresses. Allison says can't pick this one shows my figure. Look, does my belly seem bigger to you? Maybe this one makes me feel like I'm going to a ball. So is Enrique Prince Charming, Maria says? Nakeya looks at Maria and shakes her head. Looking for that perfect dress came easy for you two? Not sure what I want?

Nakeya walks over picks out one and tells Allison to try it on. This one Nakeya, it's so me? It fits your personality now, Maria says Complexted? The gown that Nakeya picked out was a tight fitted pink strapless gown with beaded trimming all along the bottom which flared out, with a matching long veil that the top has the same exact beading on it. You're going to make a Beautiful Bride. Allison turns around to face Nakeya and Maria while getting the dress says "Argentina here we come" just full of smiles. Next day

Allison starts talking to herself: I have the perfect dress, perfect location to get married and perfect groom so why am I nervous? Enrique tells Allison to hurry up, we have to meet everyone at the airport. We're going to be late Allison we have to go like now.

Allison still babbling to herself have to do one final look. Are we missing anything? Jose asked Lydia who were they waiting for?

Rafael replies looking for them facing the front door, the future Bride and Groom?

Roman tells Rafael to call them then sees them walking in,never mind.

Nakeya says and why are you two so late? Enrique points to Allison.

Rafael and Jose reply jokingly maybe it was traffic? Sure, you're right.

Announcer says now boarding flight 379 to Argentina at Gate P. Maria says well gang that's us let's get this party started?

An airport worker asked them if they needed some help getting on the plane, they said no and began loading onto the plane.

Jose replied jokenly did we bring too much stuff the plane is tilting? Allison says nervously to Enrique "I feel we are leaving something important. Enrique replies to Allison we have everything.

Rosetta asked Allison if she was ready to become a wife and mother all at the same time? Allison was about to answer but instead ran towards the bathroom and she was getting sick. Um hold that thought she yells back at Rosetta?

Lydia says aloud you got to love that morning sickness.

Nakeya then replied she's only just in the beginning stage.

Maria replies before Allison returns, she still got eight in a half month to go?

Allison started babbling to herself in the bathroom" Allison why did you get pregnant again? Oh yeah being freaky and, karma got me back for making fun of them. Allison returns, sorry about making fun of you Nakeya, Karma truly is a vindictive Bitch.

The stewardess came past and asked if any one of us wanted something to drink, something to eat or snack on or read? Everyone starts to talk all at once then she takes their order and then tells them that she will be back with their things.

Jose asked another flight attendant what movie was playing. Flight attendant replies to Transformers. Lydia asked her if she could get them some headphones.

Juan waves over here we need a couple of pairs on this side.

Flight attendant replies one moment please. Is it loud enough? They all nodded to the flight attendant yes and then Thanked her.

The flight attendant asked after passing out the stuff if there was anything else?

Jose replies, No I think we are all good, you have been very helpful.

Pilot comes over the loudspeaker saying they will be arriving in Argentina in six hours. Nakeya says I love this movie he's so sexy. Rafael replies, who's so sexy Nakeya?

Na'keya replied he is second to you, you're my first choice Rafael.

Allison asked Enrique again in a panicked voice, "are you sure I grabbed the dress and my shoes?

Enrique replies for the thousand time yes, Allison stop worrying?

Enrique then tells Allison that their wedding will be perfect.

Flight attendant comes over the loudspeaker, please buckle your seatbelts. We are about to land into Argentina's airport. The flight attendant tells them as they exit the plane thank you and watch their step and come again.

Jose says well what should we do first, go eat or meet with the father?

Enrique replies unpack then head over to the church and meet with Father Lopez to practice walking down the aisle and, who's standing next to who?

Enrique introduces everyone to Father Lopez. Good evening, nice to meet you all. Father Lopez recognizes Rosetta and Roman. Does Father Lopez know my parents? It's been a long time. Father Lopez married me and your father, Rosetta replied to Enrique. Father Lopez then asked Enrique and Allison if they were ready to get started?

Father Lopez started placing people in different spots, you three will stand here and you ladies over here.

Father Lopez is let's do a practice run and cue the music he tells his assistant Ms. Garcia. You ladies will begin walking down the aisle, when you hear this beat. I will say who gives this woman to this man. Then you will reply, we do. Then you take your seat with your wife. Then I will begin Dearly beloved it. Blah blah, blah then you will say your vows. Blah, blah, blah then you say your vows. Then you will exchange your rings. Blah, blah, blah. I now pronounce you Husband and Wife you may kiss the bride. Then you're done, any questions Father Lopez asked?

Jose says can we please get something to eat I'm starving? Dinner was good Rosetta says but let's all turn in we have a busy day tomorrow. Allison starts babbling and has to get my nails done, my hair, and then my make-up and some other stuff we can't understand. Maria asked Allison if she was alright talking to herself.

Allison replies tearing up I'm just getting overwhelmed that's all. It's happening so fast. Nakeya says, Allison it's been five months? Allison replies "I know I'm fine. Rosetta says ladies time to get up? We're up moma Rosetta. Rosetta says the lady doing our hair she's coming here to do our hair, make-up. Maria says what time sleepy sounding?

Nakeya says laughing I guess now there goes the doorbell. 5 mins?

Jose tells Maria half asleep that he will see them all at the church.

Maria asked Lydia if she could help with the kids if she was finished.

Nakeya tells Allison not to cry, she's going to smear her make-up. You're going to make a Beautiful Bride; Nakeya says come finish getting dressed?

Allison's father knocks on the door but then when Nakeya opens the door her mom comes in and stares at Allison Amazed.

Allison ten minutes to showtime, Ms. Fernandez says.

Allison is talking to her dad as they walk down the aisle reminiscing about when she was younger. My Baby girl is getting married and what a Beautiful Bride she is? Allison says Dad I'm your only girl and, do you really think I'm a Beautiful Bride? He replied yes and, you look so much like your mom on our wedding day just as Beautiful. Father Lopez started performing the ceremony who gives this woman to this Man? We Do. Dearly beloved it. Now repeat after me. I Enrique take thee Allison. Now you repeat after me. I Allison take thee Enrique. I now pronounce you Husband and Wife you may kiss your Bride.

Allison says to Enrique, we're really Husband and Wife? It seemed like a couple of minutes all that worry for nothing.

Allison told NaKeya the cake and food preparations turned out Beautifully.

Maria tells Allison that she's Simply Glowing, Allison Thanks her.

Allison is confronted by different family members just Congratulating them on their wedding. Allison whispers to Enrique. I've met so many family members but can't remember half their names? Enrique just laughs and kisses her forehead.

The wedding planner asked if the Bride and Groom would come and have their first dance.

Allison calls Enrique silly, he's singing in her ear. Everybody looked so Happy.

Look at all our grown kids with their spouses dancing, they all look so happy, as their parents talk to each other and still watch them. The wedding planner asked if all the single ladies would please gather around for the throwing of the bouquet? On the count of three. 1,2,3 Oh my god Breanna caught the bouquet? Can I get all my single guys can i get you to come up for the garter throw? Come on don't be shy? A male guest yells at another guest, hey Brandon you're not single. On the count of three 1,2,3. Are you serious

Juan says to Lydia. Well look here Randy caught the garter belt.

Well, you know what that means? Wow, time has gone by so fast it's almost one in the morning.

Enrique starts Thanking everyone who came to support him and his wife on their day, but they are heading out for their honeymoon and to continue partying without them. Enrique is asking Nakeya and Rafael if their suitcases are in the vehicle. Rafael replied all suitcases are loaded and the reservation information is in the night bag. Thanks, you two, you're both our life savers.

Nakeya replies to Allison and Enrique to enjoy their Honeymoon.

Allison asked Enrique, "so where are we going? "It's a surprise," he replied. What about our stuff there and at the house? Rafael and Nakeya along with the rest of the family have it all handled, when we come back it will be at our new home. You thought of everything? At least tried to anyway Enrique replied? Our flight will be leaving in a few hours, let's see we can wait at this hotel?

Allison tells Enrique how she loves how he touches her, makes her warm inside. Allison, you send chills down my spine every time you do that Enrique replied. Lord help me, Enrique you so crazy. That was Amazing. Come on, we're gonna miss our flight?

Announcement came over the loudspeaker now boarding flight 773 to Brazil, Rio De Janeiro at Gate T. Allison stops talking to Enrique puzzled?

Did she just say Brazil, Rio De Janeiro Gate T? Oh my God we're going to Brazil? Surprise Allison and we Are staying at the Copacabana Beach in Rio? Heard it was beautiful right next to the beach. A few hours later we go get checked in. Started unpacking where we were heading first you guessed the beach. We saw so many sand sculptures along the beach as we walked to the water. Look at this sky so blue, God it's ninety- nine degrees out here. This place is so full of bright Colors and diversity and culture. They went to eat at some cafe called Parque

Dos Patins the food was Amazing. And they noticed another beautiful beach more amazing that was near the cafe it's breathtaking. We did so much sightseeing and took so many pictures on our first day. We visited the Famous statue on Sugarloaf Mountain of The Jesus Statue. You can see way up in the clouds. Makes you think you're reaching towards the sky, and you can see the whole city of Brazil from the mountaintop. We snapped so many pictures along the mountain. We then had to travel to the next place, let's go. Later that night we saw an Awesome light and music show. The ladies are dressed in bright colors and the different types of music will make you move even if you have two left feet. Seemed like we danced the whole night away. Then we went outside, and we ran across some type of carnival or festival. Wow Enrique look at these floats get some shots of their dresses and the other floats. These decorations are Amazing. As we're watching the show we're now surrounded by the fireworks displaying along the night sky. Everything is so Festive just overwhelming to look at everything all at once because, you don't want to miss anything if you can help it. We go back and get a quick shower. Allison changed into her long hot pink dress with ruffles and put on some semi-flat heels. Enrique changed into some khaki blue shorts with some type of Hawaiian blueprint shirt and some dark sandals. Tears come down Allison's cheek, are you alright? I'm having a wonderful time, must be the hormones. Thank you it's not over yet the nightlife awaits. We started at the far end of the beach and work our way down to the other side of the beach. We danced to the different music playing, then we enjoyed sipping Exotic drinks on the patio. Looking up at the sky and watching the stars twinkle on Flamingo Beach. Taking pictures of this night and remembering how Beautiful this place was. We sat down on a bench for hours talking and just remembering the carnival from earlier and the fireworks. Listening to all the different types of music in the background, looking at the Pictures we had taken earlier and holding hands. Taken in the nighttime scenery. Meanwhile back at the house have the rest of the crew just got back home from setting up Enrique's and Allison's new home? Now they were looking at the pictures that the photographer dropped off from their wedding they were great.

Maria and Nakeya decided to call them to see how they are enjoying their honeymoon if they answer the phone?

Juan says I wonder if they will answer, let's bet? The phone rings and after three Enrique answers sounding out of breath. Rosetta and Roman laugh.

Rosetta says Hello to Allison and Enrique and, how is their honeymoon going?

Allison replies that it's breath taken and can't wait to share all the pictures they have taken. Nakeya tells Allison that they just received the wedding pictures back and that they turned out Magnificent. So, take in some more attractions, take some more pictures and, we won't take of more of your time Juan replied. Well, you're not really bothering us, we were just sitting and taking a breather catching our breath Enrique tells Juan. Well, that's nice to know Rosetta says, I was feeling bad. We all want you two to continue to enjoy your honeymoon, do more sightseeing, shop at the shops Nakeya adds. We are waiting for you two to come back. Love you both they all yelled and see you both soon.

Allison and Enrique reply back to the whole family see all you guys love you all, Bye.

Allison and Enrique are talking as they pack that next morning they leave for Sao Conrado and stay there for three days. The beaches here are so clean, the water is so clear and blue. This has to be the most beautiful beach in the world. We enjoyed the beach for two whole days. Taken in the rays we hit the water and make love in between the waves. I love you, love you back. You just can't help to get lost in the beauty of this place we made love on the beach that night. Looking up at the sky, the stars. Oh Enrlque, yes, my love If I wasn't pregnant? I would have gotten pregnant tonight and they laughed. We got dressed and headed back to our hotel. Where we finished making love with no interruptions. Good morning sleepy head, good morning love muah. What time is it? Almost noon, why did you let me sleep so long? Well, we made love almost all last night and you need your sleep. You're carrying our future son or daughter. Just don't want to miss anything. You won't know what you eat. We have a busy day. Allison put on your denim capris with the matching top, that seems to be getting snug? We're coordinating you see that, i have on my denim shorts with a matching short sleeve denim shirt and blue tennis shoes. I have a surprise, you are going to have a Spa day? I am yeah along with a shopping spree. Please don't cry Allison? What do you want to do first? It doesn't matter, the first stop is at a clothing outlet called Barra Da Tijuca famous for its enormous shopping center. Oh, the sales lady says to them. Hello, would you like to try this on, right this way?

Enrique told Allison she looked very sexy. Excuse me, I need a bigger size? How many months are you? Almost three thank you. That's it next shop? Sorry I don't like that color but nice dress. Too tight around the belly? I love your belly honey. Sorry we don't have a bigger size in that style, how about this? I love it. Allison says it's so sexy now for the shoes. It's your day, let me put these in the car be right back. The heat is getting to you. I want you to be careful. Enrique, I like those shoes with this one? Those can go with either or? True but not that color the other ones? Maybe these? Yikes make sure it's a semi-heel for that outfit. Be back going to the car again. Want to eat it's nearly five? What we have been shopping for over five hours? I am quite hungry. Then we went to the spa. after we eat? It won't be too late now it's reserved just for you. What are you craving for anything weird? Nothing special, something sweet and smothered in gravy? Good evening please be seated. May I get you something to drink. Scotch on the rocks and a virgin pina colada for my wife. Be back in a few minutes. Here you are ready to order. We would like to sample this dish, a sample of those, a warm spinach salad with bacon bit, grilled chicken topped with ranch dressing for both. Be back in twenty minutes. Don't eat so many bread sticks? Thanks, everything looks great. Would you like anything else, a refill? Please one moment here you go enjoy. Meanwhile back at the house Karim goes to Nakeya's to drop something off Gabriella runs up to give him a hug he thanks her then leaves.

Rafael runs into him as Karim leaves. Good evening love, sorry I'm running late? Dinner was great, we then put the kids to bed and, then we got ready for bed and cuddled then dozed off to sleep. That next morning, when Nakeya gets to the office, she greets Liz

and Vivian. When she looked in Maria's office, she noticed that Maria was talking to someone. A few minutes later Maria sits down in my office, and she fills me in who the mystery man was? I looked at Maria with amazement, does she truly have friends in high places? Morning ladies, morning Mr. Keymon replied to Liz and Vivian. Nakeya calls him into the office. Karim, do you know a guy by the name of but before she could finish, she was interrupted.

Liz comes to Nakeya's office door. Excuse me, Mr. Keymon your client is here? Excuse me Nakeya will talk later? Mr. Fritz, Good morning come right this way. Then the phone rang along with a fax. How can i ever Thank you, Maria says to herself?

Juan tells Maria that she just missed Allison and Enrique, they just left.

Nakeya opens the front door and sees Enrique and Allison. It surprised her they were coming around the corner.

Nakeya says welcome back you two how was your Honeymoon? We have so many pictures to show you, it was so Amazing? We started glancing at the pictures. After we had dinner not too many minutes afterward.

Allison and Enrique said their goodbyes, they were tired and left.

Nakeya meets Maria in the garage where she was dropping off something for Rafael. When she showed me the letter from Karim addressed to Maria and myself. Stating he was leaving to work things out with his wife. That next when we walked in we noticed Liz? Looking as if she lost her best friend?

Nakeya asks Liz what's wrong with her? Then Liz begins to tell us that she was having an affair with Karim, and he decided to leave to work things out with his wife.

Maria replies sarcastically after Liz left; well, I didn't see that coming. Liz told Vivian she was going to miss him; Vivian just hugged her.

Nakeya replied to Maria, Karim leaving came out of nowhere? Would not have guessed them hooking up, Maria adding.

Nakeya suggested to Maria they half up his clients and go from there luckily, he had no new clients lined up. Guess we can ask Allison to fill in if we need help until we hire someone else? Months had passed and we got a phone call one day finally from Karim.

Nakeya answered the phone, Liz was on break. Karim was on the phone. Hello stranger Nakeya says, he tells me how he and his wife were expecting a baby and had been living in Italy.

Karim asked if Nakeya and Maria could join him via phone to help on a new case together if they didn't mind? It was too much for one, so they agreed to help. It takes them a few weeks to prepare for their first court hearing. That first day we went home with our heads hurting from thinking about different strategies. I would get so frustrated

Rafael would sleep in the kids room and Jose would go down to the basement, or if he heard us zoom call he would then take the boys and stay at the hotel just to get some Peace.

Nakeya and Maria go back to court, and we start our deliberations. First Maria gives some insight to the jury, then I'm supposed to give some insight using a possible motive.

Back at the office Nakeya loudly in her office says court is draining. I just want to go home get a stiff drink and just drop? Rafael and the kids always make me feel better. Always gives me that extra push whenever I need it. Whenever I can't sleep, I call Maria and talk about strategies. Then Rafael says something that had stumped us for weeks.

Nakeya gets a light bulb moment and shares it with Maria. We both just scream, "are you serious? That next morning Maria, is that it? What's its Nakeya, Maria looks at her puzzled not following you? Then i tell her when we entered the courtroom, we huddled up.

Nakeya goes outside to call Rafael and says, you're a Genius? What you said last night made us look over the original transcripts and something had been overlooked the first time it was reported.

Nakeya and Maria that night both slept like babies. That next morning, we met with our client and discussed what we discovered. Our clients remember saying something but never agreed to such doings. Which now explains why the signatures don't match on the documents the other person has in their possession. The Judge enters the room all silent then asks Nakeya and Maria to approach the bench?

They approached the bench, Your Honor with our new findings we have changed our plea. The Judge ruled in our favor. We Won that case. We took the whole entire family out that night. Celebration on our big Victory. We were drinking some wine and eating some type *of seafood then all of a sudden, we stopped talking and started listening?*

We heard on the news there was a shooting and it left two people dead and, one in serious condition. We all felt saddened to hear this about my beloved college buddy fighting for his life, but his wife and baby girl had been pronounced dead at the scene. A month passes and Nakeya wonders how our friend is doing?

Nakeya and Maria are talking in her office when we got an unexpected visit from Glen the guy from college who lost his family.

Nakeya gives him a long hug and expresses to him our condolences. I need your help to investigate the deaths of my wife and daughter? He starts telling us about the stuff that had transpired before the accident.

Nakeya and Maria both looked at each other, and agreed we would help. So, we both agreed to take the case. You realize you handed me a check for five thousand. Glen replied to start if you need more just ask. He smiled at Nakeya then left the office.

Nakeya and Maria start working on his case for a few hours.

Nakeya excuse me your husbands are here. Come here to take you three sexy ladies for lunch? Good I'm starving Maria said let's go. Nakeya tells Liz and Vivian to hold our calls and they replied enjoy.

Liz and Vivian continue to work on getting the information about Mr. Johan's wife the previous client, then begin work on Glen's.

Reservations for Romas party of six, Rafael asked at the desk.

Greeter replies to Rafael please follow me right this way.

Nakeya replied we would like some white wine to start all for four and a virgin mai tai for my sister-in-law?

Jose replied to Maria having a hard day at work it's only eleven thirty? We are investigating the deaths of Glen's family.

Maria drank her glass of wine straight down then asked for another then replied, yeah that was so sad.

Maria and Na'keya told them without going into too much detail the guys agreed that we are doing the right thing.

Nakeya orders for everyone I would like to get the shrimp pasta with snow peas, got Maria the warm spinach salad with bacon ranch dressing, ordered Rafael and Jose carne asada with jalapeno sauce. Three more orders of wine then we go back to work.

Maria asked Liz if we had any phone calls and handed her the messages and said the boxes arrived hours ago. We will see you when we're back from lunch.

Nakeya tells Maria thinks we should call Karim for some help?

Liz replies already did and he will be here by seven o'clock tonight or the next day? How did she know to call him, Maria replied to Nakeya? I'm just that good, Liz replied. Vivian says bye to the girls as they both walk out. Nakeya and Allison go into the office and re-read some notes. Maria went to her office looking up and copying items, also looking up other things. Then all of a sudden, we heard a noise and ignored it.

Nakeya and Allison heard that noise again, this time they both stopped, walking towards the front door, oh my Liz. Sorry my hands were full; Maria opened the door. The last of the boxes, thanks Liz now I'm gone.

Allison says what is all this stuff and, why is it so much of it?

Maria replied it says papers to look at to help with this case?

Nakeya says, it's going to be a long night. God does this phone ever stop ringing? We were busy reading then we looked up.

You girls ready for a dinner break? Jose and Rafael were staring at us smiling, we smiled back.

Nakeya and Maria begin to eat while Enrique checks on Allison.

Rafael tells Nakeya what they brought warm spinach salad with Bacon ranch dressing, Mexican casserole, snow peas and, for dessert a homemade lemon pound cake. Rosetta is always looking out for us; Nakeya says wiping her mouth.

They all started cleaning up the conference room where they ate their dinner. and go home. Liz had joined us but left before dessert.

Nakeya tells Maria and Allison we pick up where we stopped reading. The very next morning Nakeya brought breakfast and went back at it.

Nakeya tells Maria to check out the picture of Mr. Moore and Glen?

Nakeya says to herself, how is he involved in this? This can't be good, then there's a couple more with Glen, Alex and Glen's wife?

Nakeya and Maria begin to read the letters that are in the box, this case just got more interesting?

Allison says it sounds like she had a double life or knows a lot of people? Maria starts to call some of her friends in her office. Nakeya are you alright Allison asked because Alec's name came up and your past? I'm cool takes more than that to shake me up, girl I'm cool no worries.

Maria tells Nakeya that she has some of her friends from work coming in to get A feel of how she was.

Allison tells Maria and Nakeya that she had some family coming in that called her back.

Allison says if she was an Heir to the Ambassador then Glen may be compensated for her untimely death or target?

Nakeya daydreams on her way home about Alec? Nakeya waved at Maria before she turned. What is the connection between these three? Maybe i should be straight and ask Glen? Why am I still thinking about this man? Rafael was asleep when I came in, so I went to my office after my shower to read some more when he noticed the light in my office.

Nakeya you are burning the midnight oil he asked. No just had to make a quick note before I forgot off to bed.

Nakeya replies but I still have some time for my favorite man. Rafael calls me but I don't hear him had my mind elsewhere. Nakeya I'm talking to you? Nakeya you hear me, no sorry must have zoned out. The kids are asleep, are you hungry or want a snack with your tea? Nakeya saw a figure or something by the tree to cause her to pause. Looks like you saw a ghost. Kissed him good night and said to myself if he only knew.

Nakeya is talking to herself dreading going down this path that Mr. Moore is involved better yet comes across him?

Nakeya was still talking to Rafael and herself talking about how great. dinner was. Making love seems to help you relax so we made love and it did. That's my job to make sure you and our kids are safe. So why when we were finished was, I still having that conversation in my head?

Rafael suggested after this case maybe get away for a few days not really listening responded, sounds like a plan babe. The next day in the office Rafael visits to check on me, suddenly gets lost in my train of thoughts.

Nakeya zones out glanced out the window to get her head straight. Oh, my No? You alright girl? Your hand is bleeding. I broke my glass and glanced back out. He's gone? Who's gone? Neither mind thought I saw something but my mind is racing?

Nakeya asked herself if I just saw Alec again this time at the office. And if so, what is he up to? Why is he involved and can't tell Rafael last time was hell for us? But little did I know that glazing right across the street from me was Alec staring at me thinking about his next move?

Nakeya and Rafael go back to the house and, as they're pulling up, don't notice the window has been smashed and broken out. We get out and, at first, they're talking and, then he stops mid-sentence, then I follow his eyes in what he is looking at.

Nakeya grabbed her mouth in shock and couldn't believe what she saw?

Nakeya then asked herself who could have done this?

Rafael once inside starts pacing the floor and he starts to place something on it to keep things out. I will get the window fixed in the morning.

Nakeya doesn't ask any questions, just lies in his arms and thinks to herself, please don't let that girl be out of jail and did this to get back at us because she went to jail?

Rafael tells Nakeya, "Don't worry I will find out who did this, and they will be sorry.

Nakeya and Rafael both checked on the kids and went to bed. Nakeya does but it was hard for me to fall asleep thinking about what happened? What I found out and what I thought I saw? When I finally dozed off it was time to get up.

Nakeya started dreaming about Alec and what happened with them at the hotel on the business trip, then I thought I saw him in the room as I started to wake up and started screaming and jumped up.

Rafael says Nakeya baby you're having a bad dream, he holds me you're safe. He kissed me on the forehead, and he held me in his arms, I felt safe, but it had me thinking?

Nakeya and Rafael are talking to each other and replying to the next morning he asked me what I was dreaming about? I lied and said I was being eaten by a big dinosaur. You have the weirdest dreams no more late-night eating for you. It must have given you nightmares, I said yeah maybe.

Nakeya and Rafael both go downstairs, and mom has the kids already fed and they are in the living room watching television. The window people are working on putting the new window back in.

Rosetta answered the phone hello, hello don't call here and hung up the phone?

Rafael asked who was that, Mom?

Nakeya doesn't say anything and continues to sip some coffee.

Rosetta says it's been happening since eight this morning. I can hear them breathing and they don't say anything.

Rafael says I am going to see if Mona has gotten out and see if she did where she is? But I am going to report this to the police.

Rosetta says do you think we really should Rafael?

Rafael replies, hell yeah, I need to keep my family safe. You're going to be ok getting to work Nakeya?

Nakeya replied yeah Allison is going to pick me up.

Allison wakes up and says morning to you all.

Rafael replies speak of the devil, and she appears laughing?

Allison tells Enrique your family is talking about me again.

Enrique replies, babe they are your family to remember? And he kisses her on the cheek as she playfully smacks Rafael.

Allison asked Nakeya, "are you ready? Yeah, let's go got to get some coffee for work.

Nakeya tells Allison that Maria will be late as we start making our way to the store. Back at the house Rafael calls the police station and talks to the officer who arrested Mona, the crazy psycho from his past that still carried a torch for him. The officer said she had been released early for good behavior. But once he reported what happened he asked if he had proof, it was her? The cop replied he would take the report and do some investigation. Later on, that day as I was working I got a weird feeling and started looking around?

Na'keya says it felt as if someone was watching us. I just felt uneasy the whole day. Maria caught me looking out the window.

Maria asked Nakeya girl what is wrong with you? Nothing, it doesn't look like anything you worried about the broken window at home? I just talked to my brother, and he told me what happened? Are you alright? My brother is going to make sure the family is safe from whoever did it? All the family will make sure the house is safe from any intruders. We start talking about the case and Allison comes in with some news. Girls look at what I just found out, Allison finally joined me and Maria at our firm full-time.

Nakeya says Allison has only been with us for four months, but she's been in heaven sent doing our research when we are doing other stuff or on another case. I really don't want to work on this because my past is coming up.

Nakeya asks herself why is Alec's name coming up in this case and will I have to interview him if he is a witness? Do I really want to go back down that path? I keep my concerns to myself, and I begin reading silently. I didn't even notice Rafael behind me. I jumped; God don't do that babe you scared me.

Rafael and Nakeya begin talking and replying to each other. Sorry I scared you? You seem preoccupied all is well? Yeah, I was just reading some paperwork about this case we are working on. You seem tense? I'm fine. You sure? I said I'm fine. You don't have to bite my head off? The window is fixed you don't have to be scared. You don't have to worry, and he comes over there and hugs me. I hugged him but I'm not thinking about what I read. Me and the boys are going to pick up a few things and we will see you all back at the house. I called mom to see how the kids are, and she told me that they are playing in the playroom. As we started walking to the car a black car drives past us slowly and it scares Nakeya.

Rafael calls Nakeya, she just looks over and just pauses.

Rafael says Nakeya snaps out of it and I get in the car, and I'm quiet the rest of the way home.

Nakeya starts having a private conversation with herself in her head. Family dinner is always a great time. I looked around and see a big, wonderful family. I just can't help wondering if what I saw was real or is my mind playing tricks on me?

Rafael asked Nakeya again, "you've been quiet all night, you hardly ate? Are you still thinking about your nightmare?

Nakeya replies no sweetheart just tired.

Rafael tells Nakeya I will draw you a bath to help you relax. Sounds good, a nice bubble bath.

Nakeya starts taking off my clothes and I hear him talking but I'm not really listening. I hear him in the background then all of a sudden, silence.

Rafeal is talking still, and Nakeya is zoning in and out of the conversation? Keya, huh you hear me calling you? Um yeah, I was taking off my clothes to get into the hot bubble bath? I don't even remember saying bye to the family.

Nakeya starts to get relaxed and dozes off but jumps up because of what was in her dream? Quickly puts on her night clothes.

Rafael asked Nakeya how her bubble bath was? Is it what the Dr ordered?

Nakeya replied, still having a private conversation in her head. Yeah honey, thank you. But I hate to lie to him. I don't want him to worry about me. He has enough to worry about. I don't want to make him worry over a silly dream I've been having. I need to understand my dreams before I even begin to figure out how to tell him about my dreams about the guy who almost ruined our happy home?

Nakeya that night had another dream. This time they are on the plane, and he is starting to reach between my legs whispering in my ear and then we are back in the hotel room. Where we first had our sexual encounter. I could feel him inside me. I woke up and began to cry but careful not to wake him up. He rolls over and puts his arm around me. I just lay there and try to feel the love I have for my husband. But ever since I started having these dreams it feels like I'm cheating on him all over. Only in my dreams or shall I say my nightmares? When we made love this morning, I closed my eyes, and I thought about how great it was to make love to my husband? So why was part of me thinking about my time with Alec? While in the shower I scrubbed my skin like it was dirty? I felt dirty like I did when the first incident with Alec occurred on the plane and then in the room. I scrubbed myself raw and started bleeding. I didn't even eat breakfast. I just wanted to get to work and work on the case.

Nakeya gets to work before Maria and Allison arrive. An hour later.

Allison says to Nakeya you're in here early.

Nakeya replies yeah decided to read over some stuff before court.

Allison says on the other case we had been working on before we got this complicated one. We are in court and have a flashback. I just shake it off. We are finishing up with the last testimony and we are told they are going to deliberate. We break for an hour for lunch. As we start walking down the steps from the courthouse. We are just talking when we hear in the distance loud talking and Nakeya, Allison and Maria all turn to look and it's a group of guys talking about sports. But before I turned to get in the back of the car, Nakeya noticed a familiar face and gasped.

Nakeya just froze again in disbelief. Did I just see Alec again?

Maria noticed Nakeya just staring into space. You alright let's go?

Nakeya replied having doubts um yeah, but she wasn't. I thought I saw Alec? And that thought scares me just like my nightmares I've been having. Back at the courthouse Nakeya tries to calm down.

Nakeya tries to get her thoughts clear and then the court is back in session. We started to have our last argument when my Karim came in and he whispered in my ear, and I gasped. Nakeya says your Honor may I approach the bench. And then the judge says the court will reconvene on Monday at eight?

Maria, Allison and Karim all looked at me as if I was crazy?

Nakeya tells them, I will explain back at the office. When we got back to the office, she shared the new information that Karim just shared.

Nakeya, Allison, Maria and Karim find out that it was even more complicated. Losing track of time, Maria says it's almost six and still have to get dinner started? Maria says maybe get some fast food tonight. Wow didn't realize it was late. We got in our cars and went home.

Nakeya dreams about being back in her hometown but then all of a sudden sees Mona? And she yelled something at me, and I jumped up.

That morning, we decided to go in late since we left late. The police came knocking on the door. Rosetta opens the door to let them in.

Rafael is talking to the cops. Rafael then gets a puzzled look then heads back towards the kitchen. I walked up to him and asked what was that all about?

Cops tell Rafael Mona has gone missing and, they asked him if any of us have heard or seen her? He also asked if they had any leads about who broke our window.

Cops replied to Rafael that a neighbor saw someone in the backyard. It was dark so she didn't see their face.

Jose and Rafael were talking at first. Jose came in and he whispered something to Rafael then they all left? Then I saw Enrique and Juan come back five minutes later, no Rafael?

Rosetta tells Nakeya whatever its is doesn't look good? The Romas's boys look like they are on a mission?

Nakeya says to herself, "think I'm working from home? I'm just drained, don't I feel like putting on clothes?

Maria, Allison and Karim all must have been feeling the same way because an hour later we made a zoom call. Talking about our next plan of action in our pajamas at our homes. Nakeya asked Maria and Allison if something happened. They all stopped talking and the screen went black. Why did they rush over here like they did, Nakeya asked herself as she saw their cars pulling up?

They look just as confused as I was. We heard the basement door open, and wanted to see what's going on?

Rafael tells Nakeya nothing to worry about, but that only makes me worry more. I don't push but I know something is wrong, just not sure what?

Nakeya walking and sensing something is wrong. The next day as Nakeya walks into work noticed the look on Maria's face. What happened now?

Maria tells Nakeya sorry he's dead. Who's dead? Glen, they found his body at his home in his master bedroom with a single shot to the head at close range.

Nakeya starts to cry, and Allison, Maria and Karim gather around to console her. I just saw him trying to get help from his family and now he's gone. Rafael came in while she was crying. Nakeya didn't even notice him. She turned around and there he was. He just opened up his arms and I knew that things would be better.

Rafael tells Nakeya maybe she should take the day off. No babe i can't go home. Well take some time off, he was your friend from college. Fine but I will work on the case from home but not today? Nakeya leaves her car there. We rode to get some lunch then went home. Glen's sister had called and left a message on my house phone. She tells me that he left something for me and that she would let us know whenever the arrangements were.

Nakeya kissed the kids and went to her room. Rafael knew I was about to break. He just held me inside his arms and said remember the good times. And before long closed my eyes.

Nakeya had a nightmare but can't remember it all. All she remembers is that she jumped and scared Rafael out of his sleep. Are you alright Nakeya?

Nakeya tells Rafael sure while holding her chest to try and catch her breath. What had you tossing and turning in your sleep Keya? Was it about the news you had about your friend? Yeah, that's not an easy thing to get off your mind? I just saw him in my office now he's gone. Well, if you think about it he is with his wife and daughter? I'm sure he is happy. I'm going to get some apple-cinnamon tea then go back to bed, promise. He kissed me on the forehead, and he laid back down. I'm here if you want to talk or just need a hug.

Nakeya saw a shadow by the kitchen window and started screaming. Rafael came running down the steps and when I told him what I saw. Rafael and Roman both went outside and walked around the house. Nakeya called the cops and they sent someone out to get our report. Officer Kimbo took my statement and saw my husband. He had a look in his eyes like he had the other time. We finally went back to bed at five and later on that morning he started calling to get cameras and more security around the house.

Nakeya and Rafael a few days later went to pay their respects to Glen's family. Inside my head thoughts and memories of us from years ago came flooding my mind. And tears just flowed. The homecoming service was beautiful, I must admit.

Nakeya talks to Glen's sister and consoles her. Your brother would be so proud. If you need anything, please don't hesitate to call me anytime. I could hear Rafael talking in the background with Glen's other siblings. My brother always said you were the one who got away? Oh really half laughing he always told me that he wanted you to have his favorite necklace if something happened to him. This is the necklace that we got on our senior trip to the Bahamas tears fell. This letter will explain everything. I will give you a couple of days and we will talk. My brother found out something and think it got him killed? My heart dropped. I gave her a hug and we headed home but that conversation played over and over in my head.

Nakeya is thinking about an earlier conversation and thinking to herself. My brother might have gotten murdered for something he found out. It raced all night in my mind. My eyes were so swollen from the funeral. I'm kind of glad it's Saturday to get my eyes to stop swelling. Rafael took the kids out to give me some alone space. I love my husband he is thoughtful, and I love him for that. I opened up the letter and began reading it. By the time I got to the end. I was at a loss for words and couldn't believe what I was reading. My in-laws told us they were going to move to my old apartment. I understand they want privacy. It's a bittersweet moment. We need a bigger house to accommodate everyone. I'm going to miss her cooking homemade pasties in the middle of the night when she can't sleep. As the men transfer their stuff to my old apartment, Nakeya tears up a moment.

Nakeya decided to talk to Maria, Karim and Allison about Glen's letter the next day at work. They looked at me as if I were crazy. What they just read you can't make this shit up. We are talking about the letter and the guys come into the office conference room where we are talking.

Rafael asked Nakeya what are you three talking about? A new case but we can't discuss it.

Rafael tells Nakeya let's go out and eat dinner. Mom and Dad have all the grandbabies besides you ladies look stressed? So, we all get dressed up, go eat at a fancy restaurant and then go dancing.

Nakeya tells Rafael have to admit having a blast just what the Dr ordered. Because it's going to be a tough few weeks ahead. Dancing with my husband and spending time with him is great. We are all talking, smiling and enjoying adult conversation. Nakeya glances in a different direction and sees someone in the shadows staring at them?

Rafael asked Nakeya if anything was wrong, she didn't reply or just continued to talk.

Nakeya doesn't want to mess up their night, so she doesn't look at that spot, but I still have that feeling that we are being watched?

But by whom I don't know. Monday morning blues, uh.

Maria, Allison, Karim and Nakeya all started looking into some stuff Glen was doing before he got killed? I had Maria re-trace his last week? While the rest of us read and looked at the things in the boxes.

Allison looked into his last hours and talked to some of the people. And if we find something we might have to get his sister to reopen his case?

We talked to quite a few people and saw a car following us. I didn't say anything at first. I just analyzed and paid more attention to our surroundings.

Nakeya calls Maria and told her the same thing.

Nakeya begins talking to herself again while reading stuff. Was he really losing his mind and just having thoughts and because of the pain of losing all his family he killed himself?

Nakeya, Maria, Allison and Karim are all reacting? Hearing some of his last conversations about his family was heartbreaking. Nakeya steps away as Karim continues to read his notes.

Maria stayed and wrote down the information on the notepad? Allison gave me a hug and asked me if I was alright?

All of us meet back up at the office around one and we just decide to share what each of us have found out and decide which way to move next?

All of us decided to break early. We all waved at each other as we headed out. Nakeya noticed a light left on so went back in and turned it off.

Nakeya turns to leave and sees a shadow near the office window. I stand still for a minute to see if I can see who it is. Keya you in there?

Ralphie babe you scared the hell out of me? Well, I was worried you didn't answer your phone? Must be in the car, sorry Nakeya says.

Nakeya and Rafael are talking and asked were you just creeping around the window babe? No just saw your light on came over, thought you were going to burn the midnight oil and thought about bringing you all some dinner? So, you just weren't around the bay window? No just pulled up. Did you see someone there? Then we looked out and saw someone running away. He wanted to run after him.? No maybe we should get some more security and motion sensor lights to detect movement here as well. We headed home and now that has him more on edge. What pushed me over the edge was what I was thinking or saw earlier?

Nakeya dreamed about Alec again. I could feel his hands all over me and feel him inside me.

Nakeya tries to clear her head while talking to herself? Nakeya goes downstairs to clear her mind. Why am I having dreams about Alec? I have to admit never felt that way with Ralphie. Alec just had a way of caressing me. I love my husband and can't find myself having sex with Alec again? But have to admit, on the other hand Alec made me feel things never felt?

Rafael tells Nakeya he will call to get more lights and security around the office. Thank you, babe. If you're going to be late? I will call you so you can meet me. Mom watches the baby while we work, and the other kids are at school.

Nakeya kisses Rafael and they drive to their jobs.

Nakeya tells Maria, Allison and Karim good morning to meet in her office. She tells them she stopped to get coffee and tea along with some muffins so they can talk about what we found on a full stomach. As we start talking about the case and sipping coffee. We didn't notice a delivery had come to the door Maria goes and signs *for it.*

Karim says, "What is it, who's it for?

Maria replies to Karim doesn't know? It doesn't have a name on it?

Maria opens up the package slowly. It has a note she reads it. Glen was loved by many so decided to share this information with you. Be careful don't let his death be in vain.

Allison says aloud listen to this. According to his date book states Glen had a meeting with Alec at one that Tuesday and the next week he's found dead on a Friday? Nakeya replies does it say what the meeting was about? Maria replied not sure what it was all about something about numbers that's all it says?

Nakeya tells herself "I don't want to talk to Alec let alone be around? I've been having some crazy thoughts about him and dreams. If I have to consult him where and how to contact him? But he will be my last resort?

We decided to wrap up our days in the office early until we get extra lights and security around the place for inner peace. But we always can do our work separately at home when our families allow us to?

Nakeya says Something smells good. Rafael happily says to Nakeya your home early. We are going to start leaving the office early together until we get extra security. Besides we can always work at home.

Nakeya tells Rafael look it had started snowing hard outside?

Nakeya and Rafael both say where did that come from? And it looked like it's going to stick. Well guess we're not going to the office tomorrow? We will play it by ear? Na'keya asked Rafael if she have enough time to shower before dinner was ready?

Rafael replied how about we take a bubble bath together and have some adult time? Sounds like a great ending to a stressful day.

Gabby says Mommy's here? Hey mommy's babies. Nakeya takes off my shoes, puts on my slippers and sets the table. Nakeya feeds Kaden first. Gabriella starts looking at the snow falling by the big bay window.

Nakeya says she has always loved it when it snowed. Nakeya has a quick flash being a little girl looking out the window of my childhood home watching the snow falling, then snapping back.

Nakeya and Rafael eat dinner then we give the kids their baths. But Gabriella keeps checking if it's still snowing? Are we staying off school tomorrow? Rafael begins to run the bubble bath for them?

Nakeya starts undressing and then a flashback of her exotic night with Alec popped into her head. Shake my head. Rafael noticed and asked Nakeya was she alright?

Rafael slowly kisses her neck when he enters the tub and that starts things.

Nakeya started kissing him passionately back then on his neck.

Rafael and Nakeya began making love in the tub.

Nakeya jokingly says you know this is how we conceived our son?

Rafael laughs then says round two and continues to kiss her neck.

Rafael and Nakeya dry off and get ready for bed. We slowly drift off to sleep as the snow continuously keeps falling outside. Sometime around two-thirty Nakeya makes her way to her office

and tries to get some work done.

Nakeya overheard Rafael talking to someone on the phone who sounded like a girl not his sister?

Nakeya is listening and thinking the last thing she hears is you know I love you? Did I just hear him right? He asked someone else love you besides his mom, sister, me or his daughter? Don't jump to conclusions?

He saw me and jumped?

Oh, hey baby, what are you doing? Nothing looking at the snow? Oh school is closed the kids will be happy. Are you coming back to bed? I walk back to bed he hugs me then closes his eyes.

Nakeya asked these questions in her head? But all she focused on played over and over in my head. She heard him say you know I love you? And it wasn't easy to hear that? She got more pissed the more she thought about it? Who was on the other side of that phone call? Maybe I should confront him? No, he has never cheated on me in the past but, did he do that to get back at me? And now he can't stop it? Allison is about to go on maternity leave?

Nakeya says to herself we need another lawyer here?

Nakeya and Maria wonder to ask Karim if he would like to work on maybe another permanent position there?

Karim agrees to stay so he will be here while she's on maternity leave and we don't need to find another person.

Allison and Enrique found out they are having a boy.

Nakeya and Maria plan something special for Allison? We decided to throw Allison a baby shower at the office on a non-busy day.

Vivian and Liz get her a cake and decorate the office for the arrival of a boy along with her chair.

Nakeya and Maria send her out to a made-up client as they finish setting up?

Allison enters the office. We all yell "Surprise!" She drops her drink on the floor. Allison says to us I hate you and cries. She sees all the gifts and later opens them. Nakeya told Enrique to stop passing the house and get the bigger SUV before he comes here to take the stuff for their son to their new house and fix up the nursery? Enrique brings her to work since Allison has gotten so much bigger and, now that she is on maternity leave, she can stay home and concentrate on the birth of their son?

Everyone at the office kissed her and said our so longs, not a goodbye. Nakeya tells Maria she will be back after the little man is born. Karim had just walked in the door. Karim gives Allison a gift. Please take this gift from me and my wife. Congratulations Allison.

Allison says to Karim welcome back it seemed weird at first because of the affair. But Liz was now messing around with a guy that she met from her yoga class named Hans and seemed to be in a better place. They actually seemed like a great couple.

Vivian, can you make us some coffee? It's already brewing. Great now back to work. Three of his friends from work came in and we talked to them, and we made some notes and asked them if they remember anything to please let us know.

Nakeya reached out to his sister to tell her the progress and she hit me with some news. I share this new information with my teammates and they have the same reaction as I do. I opened my mouth to say something and Liz buzzed? You have an important call on line two. So, I excuse myself they leave its Mona? Why are you calling me? I don't have much time. I'm sending you some papers that I need you to look at and you will then understand. Then before I can say anything else. The phone goes dead.

Nakeya has a long conversation with herself. Why did she call me? Who was on the phone? An old classmate from high school? Cool is she or he coming for a visit? Maybe let's go over all that we know. So as they talk they see who is involved? I put it on the whiteboard. My theory is maybe we can see what we are missing. But I still have a question mark for contact with Alec for information? And the information from Mona I haven't shared? At least not yet, it might not be anything. Seeing Alec's picture sparks a memory and Karim asks if i was ok?

Nakeya replies to Karim's question and talks for a few minutes. Yeah, it looked like you saw a ghost. It's a long story and one day I will tell you about it.

Nakeya tells Maria and Karim to pick this up tomorrow in the morning. Sounds like a plan besides we had a busy day already.

I have to remind you to pick up some mint chocolate chip ice cream and that the security people will be out here to put more cameras and lights up. Damn, I almost forgot about that?

Thanks to Ms. Vivian she lost her husband almost ten years ago. She has been a friend of the family since I was maybe eleven years old. I asked her to come out here when I first started at the old law firm then hired her for my law firm.

Nakeya saw Mona's mom Rosalie. She asked me if I had talked to her daughter? Nakeya replied, no why would she reach out to me? I stole her life with Rafael remember.

Rosalie replied to Nakeya, Mona blew that life with Rafael way before you came into the picture then she left. Wonder what she meant by that I thought? Nakeya yells I'm home opening the door.

Rafael replied shh Kaden is asleep and Gabriella is finishing up her homework. Dinner is waiting for you on the table?

Nakeya reflects that she loves the fact that he can be home with the kids if his parents can't be there. He has his brother Enrique or Uncle Carlos as we call him to rely on if he needs someone to do late hours, but Enrique has been staying close to Allison because she is due soon.

Nakeya and Rafael had all the family over to have dinner and get caught up with family business. Even though Allison has only been gone for two weeks now we hugged each other like it was a year. We were all in the big living room and the phone rang. Rosetta answered it as if she never left, then she looked at Roman with those sad eyes. Mona's dead she said in a shocked voice?

Nakeya gasped in shock from the news. The police were called when they heard her mom screaming at her apartment. They said she was shot at close range. Rafael looked so hurt so went over and hugged him. I know she used to be a friend and I'm sorry she's gone. Then a knock came at the door. Why were the police there?

The cops tell Rafael they need to ask him some questions? Mr. Romas because of what happened, and they cleared Rafael once they checked his alibi.

Nakeya is trying to make sense of the questions the cops asked her husband. Yes, they had bad blood, but he would not have hurt her. Nakeya got an email about a package that needed to be signed. It will arrive at the office tomorrow around nine and nine forty.

Nakeya is soul searching in her head about stuff. I watched my husband get very emotional about an old flame. I don't know if I wanted to ask him why he is so emotional or be understanding because we all have a past? Besides he was there when I needed him. Did he care about her more than he was letting on? Or was that the woman on the other end that he told you know I love you? I didn't question him? I did what a good wife would do. That was to hold him and tell him that you are here for him. But in my mind, I was also thinking about all this stuff that? I don't have answers to my questions about, but I have to act like nothing's wrong and still work on this case about my best friend Glen and his death or murder? It's too much to digest and hold inside.

Nakeya left early to get the package before the rest of my team got in. Nakeya passes Vivian on the way, and she doesn't see me at least

138

I don't think she did? Eyes straight on the road dead ahead.

Delivery man knocks on the door and makes me jump. Delivery for Mrs. Romas sign here please, good day.

Nakeya sees the workman for the new security tell them they are welcome to the coffee and muffins.

Nakeya started reading the letter. It was reading to me like in stereo then reading a part about Rafael? At first didn't want to read anymore but had to. I have to say it was emotional and didn't know how to feel about Mona or Rafael? Then it said something about Glen and that got my attention. I didn't even know that they knew each other. But what does my husband have to do with this? Before I could read more heard the door alarm chime. I quickly wiped my eyes and acted normal. Nakeya replied Good Morning you guys coffee and muffins in the conference room.

Karim asked Nakeya why are you here so early?

Maria and Karim reply to Nakeya it makes us feel bad.

Nakeya says you guys are fine decided to come here in case the guys came early, and they did. Besides, we have coffee and muffins in the conference room. Please help yourself. We have a zoom call in an hour so get ready. I went into my private bathroom and cried in silence. Nakeya gets a text that they are arresting Rafael.

Nakeya apologized and told Cari she had to reschedule.

Nakeya blurts out Rafael has been arrested and has to leave. Maria leaves with her and calls Juan who is already en route to the police station. Rosetta has kids because they picked him up at home.

Nakeya and Maria arrive at the station, and they see them leading him somewhere in handcuffs? Excuse me, excuse me can we get some help over here?

The older gentleman replied wait your turn. Wait my turn do you see anyone else in here? Then out comes a familiar face. My dad's friend Mr. Barry. Nakeya, that you Dear? Yes Sir, it's me, Mr. Barry. Can you please help me? Wait here and I'll see what I can do. I went back over towards Maria and Juan then saw Rafael coming out with Mr. Barry.

Nakeya asks Rafael if they hurt him. Are you alright? What happened for them to arrest you?

Rafael replies while holding Nakeya I'm fine just want to go home Gabriella is probably having a fit.

Mr. Barry tells me that he is free to go home. We get home and Rosetta and Roman and the rest of the family are all waiting to hear what happened. He begins to talk, and my phone vibrates. I jumped because I totally forgot that I put it on vibrate.

Alec texted Nakeya you still look amazing. I glanced at it and put it away.

Nakeya looks at the number but doesn't recognize the number. Alec texted Nakeya again? I'm closer than you think? Now this is getting weirder? I see you Nakeya almost dropped the phone and closed my curtain. I saw a hooded person by the tree? I'm tripping looked again it's gone.

Nakeya starts thinking about all the stuff inside her head. Keya what do you think? Um yeah sounds like a plan not even concentrating on what she agreed with? He started making plans for a weekend getaway just the two of them. That morning, Cari zoomed with us in the conference room, and we added more information about Glen. Then we said our goodbyes and we all looked at each other? Nakeya, what have we got ourselves into? Not only are we working on this case about Glen. We also have other cases that are not as complicated. But it takes time to do some investigations. It's always *something to look up or read.*

We didn't do any work on Glen's, but we always found time to make notes about it.

Nakeya replies cluelessly not remembering that following weekend? Nakeya walked in and he said we can leave after you take your shower? Huh did you forget what I asked you? The kids are with their Godparents. We are taking a quick weekend getaway so I can get some alone time with my wife. Who has been working way too hard. I got in the shower then got dressed. I'm glad the snow melted too. He had put our night bags in the car.

Nakeya called Maria to check on the babies while Rafael was driving. Maria says enjoy your time away, the babies are fine and hung up.

Nakeya and Rafael went to some bed and breakfast. It's like a few miles away but the place is beautiful.

Nakeya and Rafael are walking in the hotel to get checked-in. We go into our room. The room is amazing a king size bed with a canopy top, a seventy-five-inch television with surround sound, a small kitchenette with a mini fridge and mini bar. We have a balcony if we want to eat outside with a mini table set but in the far corner was our master bathroom with a huge jacuzzi tub shaped as a heart. There will be no talk about work from either of us. I just want to enjoy my beautiful wife without our kids. Besides you need to relax. Nakeya is thinking about what she read and heard, and she is having a private conversation with herself. I am with my husband whom I love and adore. So why am I still thinking about the letter Mona sent me before she died? And all the other stuff I found out? I tell you why because women don't stop thinking about stuff until it makes sense, or we get answers, but will I be able to stomach the answers of the questions? I have it inside my head or will they destroy

141

our happy home? On our first night we went out to a little Italian deli and took it back to our room and sat outside on the balcony and watched the local people pass by. We also heard the local drunkards greeting us. We even heard some music coming from around the corner and we danced to the music as they played our favorite song. He fell asleep around three and lay in his arms. I was still thinking about the information I have been given and honestly don't know what I'm going to do if this information doesn't go as planned? I turned off my mind and finally fell asleep to get woken up by a loud crack of lightning. Rained hard all day and we had to have our breakfast delivered to us. Well so much for going to take a walk and explore but maybe we can go exploring later on this afternoon. We eat and then get back in bed fool around a bit, watch tv, then fool around like we are teenagers that are waking up from prom night.

Rafael looks babe the rain has stopped, good race you to the shower? Then we put on some warm clothes and some comfortable shoes and begin our exploring. There are so many antique shops we go to almost everyone just to look around. I brought something could not resist. Allison calls but doesn't answer. Texted her back, I'm enjoying my husband text you later? Then he came across a shop that had all types of snow globes from different states. He brought five then he looked at me. What have I had to? Just shook my head and laughed. They were calling my name. Sure, they were let's go get some lunch Ralphie? Looks like you worked up an appetite. Yeah, I did not for food? You're so nasty, I smacked his arm.

Nakeya and Rafael call the kids to see how they are doing. Kaden is crawling around, and Gabriella is playing princess dress-up with the girls. She always has fun over there, she hates to leave.

Rafael and Nakeya are talking and really enjoying each other. Maybe when we get back in the room we can playhouse? No let's play cops and robbers? What has gotten into you? It must be the fresh air from the mountains? I love the new you. Oh yeah, it's frisky. You know this can lead to other things? You mean if I kiss your neck like this? Yeah, it can lead to other stuff? Are you scared? You should be very afraid? I finally wasn't thinking about what was on my mind just enjoying making love to my sexy husband? I really enjoy how he makes me feel. Rafael, Rafael where are you? Where did you go? I got us some dinner. It's really pouring out there again. I could have gone with you. It's fine besides that you looked peaceful as you slept. I didn't want to disturb you. Let me heat it up. You open the bottle of chilled wine and watch the rain come down. Enjoy the last night together before we go back to reality? We should do this more often? Yeah, it would be nice just the two of us. What did you get that smells delicious? Brown rice, roast beef with sweet and sour sauce, greens with potatoes, and for dessert your favorite, chocolate cheesecake with raspberry drizzle. You are on the right path for a passionate night? Oh yeah then I will work on making it happen. Making love in the tub is so romantic, washing each other and enjoying each other just like the first time we met. Well back to reality but I will be so happy to see the kids. Yeah, I missed them. Love you babe and thank you for my quick getaway. Anytime babe just to get you unstressed.

Nakeya says Kaden think Daddy missed you more than Mommy did? Nakeya asked Gabby was she ready to go?

Nakeya thanks Maria and Jose for watching the two kids for them?

Juan replies to Nakeya we don't mind besides we love spending time with them. Gabby kissed her aunt Maria and uncle Jose and see you later uncle Juan and aunt Lydia who were visiting.

Juan and Lydia kissed Gabriella and Kaden goodbye. See you all later then they left.

Nakeya tells Rafael she was going to put Kaden down to bed.

Nakeya asks Rafael if he could get Gabriella ready for bed?

Gabriella replied I can get ready all by myself? I'm a big girl now?

Nakeya starts unpacking the suitcase, then hears Rafael and Gabby?

Gabby asks her Daddy, "did he got her something? Maybe here you go Gabby. Wow this is Bonita [beautiful] Thank you Daddy. I will put it on my dresser. Good night, night Princessa [princess]. Night Gabby, night Mami [mommy], Te Amo [love you].

Nakeya tells Rafael, Kaden has his bottle and he will be fast asleep soon.

Rafael says good so then maybe I can put you to sleep? Oh yeah love that night gown on you Keya. I can't wait to take it off of you?

Nakeya and Rafael heard Gabby say eww that's yucky?

Nakeya and Rafael started laughing. When I go to the bathroom checked on Kaden to make sure he is fine? Sound asleep drooling.

Nakeya says I'm glad you made his room attached to our master bedroom so it's easy for me to breastfeed him but tonight he got his bottle.

Nakeya tells Rafael when he wakes up for his four o'clock feeding will breastfeed then.

Nakeya looked over her emails for work fears she might have missed something while they were gone? But I don't have to worry because I have a great team. Nakeya thought to herself, "I'm glad Karim stayed on permanently. We all work well together besides Allison likes him and she doesn't get along with anyone easily.

Nakeya reads with a puzzled look on her face. What is this about? Text or call me when you get to work, and I will come to your office again?

Rafael says Morning are ready to get to the office?

Rafael tells Nakeya made your lunch and I have your breakfast right here?

Nakeya says I think you like working from home? Rafael replies to Nakeya actually yes can be with my big man and send my baby girl off and I still do my work.

Nakeya says See you later cowboy and then she reached for the door

Rafael reacts to what Nakeya did before she walked out a spank on his butt? Mrs. Romas you naughty kitten. Nakeya sees the new security system punched in her code and the lights come on even though it's sunny. Besides, we can see what is going on when we're home or away? We all can even Allison is set up. Vivian and Liz Good Morning, Nakeya says as she heads to her office.

They both reply hello dear. How was your weekend getaway?

Nakeya replied much needed, and we had so much fun. We all need to get away when we are getting stressed out.

Liz tells Nakeya someone wants to speak to you?

Nakeya replies send them in. Liz replied already waiting in the office?

Glen's sis asked Nakeya how her brother's case was going?

Nakeya replied that she will explain to her more when the others get in.

Nakeya asked Ms. Liz to get our guest some coffee or tea please?

Nakeya suggests to all of them that they go into the conference room? So, we can show you what we have found out.

Maria, Nakeya and Karim take turns talking to Glen's sister about what they found out. As we start to explain to her what we have found she starts to cry. I rub her shoulder and then after we have told her everything, she just looks like we did. Shocked and even more confused so we told her what our next move was. She said keep her posted and hugged. I will be in touch.

Nakeya gets a text from the courts. When she leaves, we get a message that we need to be at the courthouse in an hour for a ruling. So, we took two cars, and we headed towards the courthouse.

Nakeya, Maria and Karim are all meeting with our client and we tell him what our next move is but we have to hear the ruling.

All the people in the court, including us all rise when the judge comes into the room and then we sit down.

The Judge simply says after looking over all the evidence my clients will be getting out of jail. My clients shed some tears. They have been in jail for six months. They always said they were innocent, and they were. The Judge said they would be released immediately, and they would not have a record. Their parents were so happy.

Nakeya, Maria and Karim hugged the prisoners and told them they would get out soon. Their mom shook my hand and the rest of the team. You never gave up on my kids. That's our job. When they got out they gave their parents hugs and said they just wanted to go home. That really made our day one down ten to go. Lies it's only five. I know Glen's felt like three cases into one. Back at the office we have someone waiting for us. Are you the team that is working on Mr. Glen's case?

Nakeya replied yes and you are? His wife she replied? Maria says not thinking his wife is dead and his daughter?

The woman in the office replied to Maria. I was married to him, here is our marriage license. Please come in? Karim and Maria were on it only looking at Nakeya.

Karim says to Maria after they left the room with Nakeya. He was obviously living a double life? But does his sister know about her?

Nakeya gets Maria to contact the office of where this marriage took place?

Karim contacts his sister, and he leaves a message she doesn't answer.

Nakeya tells Maria and Karim after looking at the picture in Amazement. They have a little boy, there is no denying that he is Glen's.

Nakeya asks her some questions and she replies? They have the same smile and eyes. I tell her to give me a good number and address to get a hold of her with anything that comes up with his case ? I asked her where she was when they had his funeral. She was back in Greece. Her Mom had taken ill, and she went to care for her. Glen said he had to take care of some business here. She got worried when he didn't call or text her back and she found out he died by watching the news.

Nakeya gave her condolences and said that one of us would be in touch if we needed any more information.

Nakeya goes over in her head what she has so far. So now I have another wife, another child and the stuff Mona gave me before her death? And on top of that why or how is my husband involved?

Maria says Nakeya I don't think you knew Glen at all, two wives and two kids. Nakeya, Maria and Karim add our newfound information on our white board. And pick our minds thinking about different scenarios. They all ask each other about the scenarios and if they make sense. Can they work sure it could work but which one of them happened? Or was it totally something we hadn't thought about?

Karim says great lunch is here. We break for lunch, but we still talk about different scenarios. We clean up and go back to trying to role play and see what we might have missed? If only we knew what Alec has to add?

Nakeya stopped in her tracks with a blank stare? His name just makes her freeze?

Maria says to Nakeya, "I'm sorry if it brings up bad memories?

Nakeya replies to Maria No it's fine just given me a minute?

Karim says but how would we even get a hold of him better yet would he talk to us?

Nakeya suddenly says let's pick this back up in the morning?

Nakeya tells Maria and Karim good evening you guys?

Nakeya begins to lock up and sees someone looking into the office window, Roman? Nakeya asks her father-in-law, looking confused? Why are you here? How did you get here? Do you need a ride home? Roman replied get in and I will drop you off. Where was the car that we gave him? So what brings you to the office? I saw your light on? I missed Maria by five minutes and saw her on the interstate.

Nakeya says well there you are Roman. Tell Rosetta and he gets out of the car.

Nakeya comes into the house and says hi to Rafael. Hey where have you been? Giving Dad a ride home? Really yeah, he showed up at the office? He really scared me. He must have dropped off the car for repairs. I told him either me or you could pick him up?

Rafael asks Nakeya how was work? Nakeya replies smiling work was great and how was your day? Rafael smiles after hearing the news. Good, the boys that were in jail for six months were finally released and no record.

Nakeya and Rafael are still talking. That's great news. I know you are pleased, yeah, we were all happy. I have some bad news now, what? We have to go out of town on business for a job. Enrique is not going. I'm going to take Carlos. He knows the job he has been working with us for some years, besides he taught me some things I didn't know. When do you leave? In the morning early like five? How long will you be gone? Maybe three or four days. You and the kids will be fine besides you have all these cameras and we both can access it. So can the security place you and my babies are always being watched. Give me a kiss. I'm going to miss you? Call me when you get to the hotel, so I know you two made it. Love you

Nakeya says while waving. Hey Carlos, hey NaKeya later. The car disappears out of her eyesight.

Nakeya shakes her head reading this text she has received. I went back into my office and read the email. I received it while we were away. You have to be kidding me? I look up the place and see if I can find a phone number. I called the number and told her, and they agreed to meet with me. In two hours to tell me some information. I got there and saw a familiar face? Alec but he doesn't go as Alec Moore. His new name is Nino Chaz?

Nakeya looked shocked and scared at the same time. The first thing I wanted to do was run out. But his office door closed, and he was sitting in a black leather chair facing the window. So, I didn't see him until the door closed and he slowly turned around. It felt as if I was moving in slow motion.

Alec and Nakeya are talking, he asks some questions, and she replies. Nice seeing you. Sorry I can't say the same. What are you doing here? Call me Nino? Alec, what are you trying to do? Call me Nino? Fine Nino tell me what you know so I can leave? He walks toward me, and I can't move. Do I scare you? No why do you say that? Your body language changed. I moved to the chair to sit down. Can you please tell me what I asked you about? He begins telling me and then he says something about Mona and Rafael? What does my husband have to do with this case? Have dinner with me? Are you crazy? Have dinner with me and I will tell you what you want?

149

He places his hand on my shoulder. I jerk away. Do you think about me? I think about our last time. Um Nino, how do I get in contact with you? My number is the same. You look Beautiful. Good day, Mr. Chaz. Thank you for your information. He vainly smiles at me as I rush out of that office. I won't tell that part. I will share this information minus my husband until I know more. What is my husband not telling me? Why is Mona coming up in Glen's case and my husband? That night around eight Rafael calls and talks to Gabrella and Kaden. He's starting to sing the da, da da song, and he said they got their safe and that he loved me and would see us soon. I told him I loved him also and couldn't wait to see him.

Nakeya tries to relax and thinks about her day. After I get the kids ready for bed. I take a hot bubble bath and think about everything. Then I get out climb into bed it feels so empty. My phone vibrates a new message?

Nakeya reacts with this sudden text from Alec, and she's had impure thoughts? Seeing you today makes me think about our first trip. I remember how you tasted. Delete, New message? What the hell. Thinking about you, can I see you? Delete he is crazy? Buzz. What do you want? Can I taste you again? You know I make you Bye. But I have to admit it's something about him that makes me want to tear his clothes off? Another dream about him and it's like he is right here, and I can feel everything. It's dark in the room and it's like a shadow so I jump, but I am still asleep. How would Alec, Chaz, whatever he is calling himself nowadays get into my house? It's like a fortress but I don't feel safe? Nakeya gets ready for work, take Kaden to Rosetta's and drops Gabriella off at school today.

Nakeya reacts and starts to smile after reading the message then stops then starts thinking impure thoughts again? New message, I shake my head dinner and we can talk? Why am I even thinking about having dinner with this man? I know why I want to see what he knows, and my husband is not here? If he was this conversation would not have been talked about?

Nakeya left Kaden and Gabriella with Rosetta. Told her I have to meet with a client.

Alec texted me an address and I met him there at six as he asked.

Nakeya trying not to react? God, he smells Amazing. I try not to stare at him, but he is a very sexy man can't deny that?

Nakeya interrupts Alec and tells him some things. Don't call my phone anymore? Come again? Don't call my phone or contact me after this, ever?

Alec asked Nakeya some uncomfortable questions to get her reaction and replies if any? You love how I touch you he whispered in her ear?

Nakeya tells Alec to stop. Tell me I don't have all day?

Alec and Nakeya start talking and replying to one another briefly. Come eat it's your favorite. Alec, I'm leaving? No stay? Start talking what do my husband and Mona have to do with Glen? He starts talking and he walks closer towards me. I stand there and he begins to rub my arms. I still make you nervous? Nakeya reacts to Alec. Is it something about how he says my name that sends shivers down my spine and then he whispers in my ear?

Alec asks Nakeya a question and tries to deny her feelings? But he sees them. He is still talking to her. Do you want me? My mind is saying yeah, but my mouth says. No, I don't. He begins to kiss my neck. Nakeya asks him what am I doing? It felt so good he began to go under my dress and began to play with me.

Nakeya stops him but she doesn't want to? Stop, do you really want me to, and he kisses my neck. God help me, stop.? He stops. Why are you stopping what you want? Because I love my husband?

Despite what I just allowed? I gotta go. Keya, wait.

Nakeya quickly leaves good night this can't happen again?

Alec reminds Nakeya and she gulps hard remember what I said?

Nakeya got in her car and picked up the kids and goes home.

Nakeya can't get the thoughts of Alec out her mind. She remembers how good he felt and reacts. I take a hot shower and try to get his touch off me but, part of me really wanted to feel him again? But why because my sex life with my husband is good? But sex with Alec was different? Something made it mind-blowing and exotic. Nakeya finally gets the nerve to ask Rafael the truth about what she found out. I decided to ask Rafael everything I found out about him and Glen working together years ago and the parts about Mona. I had no idea about it and if he asked who told me? I would show him the letters Mona sent me.

Nakeya is soul searching and having impure thoughts? Tossing and turning most of the night then Rafael calls?

Nakeya and Rafael talk on the phone? Hello, did I wake you? Nah I can't sleep? How is the job going? We will be coming back tomorrow afternoon. Cool. Rafael, would you tell me anything that I asked you? You wouldn't hide anything from me, right? No, I wouldn't why you ask? It's because of the case you asked me this. Yeah, I guess babies don't stress. We can talk more when I get home alright. Muah nite.

Nakeya then tears up thinking about what Alec said to her. There is no way, can't let him find out about my meeting with Alec? He would flip especially with the history we have and what almost happened again? But I need to make sure Alec doesn't tell him?

Nakeya asks Alec for a favor hoping he will. I will email him and ask him to keep our meeting secret. I hate to keep secrets from my husband

and my girls, but I can't even tell them? I have to take this to the grave. I emailed Alec and told him to do me a favor. He quickly agrees to anything for you. Keep our meeting secret?

Alec doesn't respond and Na'keya panics? He doesn't text me right away.

Nakeya gets happy but tries to be bold about her favor she asks Alec? Yeah, my Nakeya. I'm not your Nakeya promise me you will keep our meeting secret?

Alec makes some demands to Nakeya, and she reacts. I will but you have to do something for me Nakeya. What is that, Alec? What do you want from me? It won't be now but when I want it you will know. And I won't take No for an answer? Alec, wait? Click.

Nakeya tears up and in her head she says. I made a deal with the Devil. Now I'm at this man's mercy? What or when will it be and, will I be able to go with it? I feel like I made a deal with Satan all for some information that may or may not be true? And was it worth doing what I'm about to do to get information? And what will it cost me? And when will it come sooner or later? Now I'm really tossing and turning.

Nakeya thinks about her feelings. Dreams that Alec and Rafael meet up again and, heard a shot in my dream? But I don't see who gets shot? My alarm clock jolts me out of my sleep. I pray that never happens. I can't lose my husband. But I also don't want to lose Alec either? Why do I have feelings for him?

Nakeya makes the kids some breakfast. I forgot it was Saturday. No work well work from home a bit.

Nakeya gets a call from Enrique. Allison keeps on having Braxton hicks and they have been going back and forth to the hospital for the past three days.

Nakeya and Allison are talking. I say it's normal to hang in there. He will come when he's ready. Allison yells in the background. I'm ready to evict him. I laugh he's not ready yet. He will come when he's ready. He's in charge. Keep me posted? How is work? Work is stressful as always? You relax on your vacation. This is no vacation.

Nakeya and Gabby finish eating. Gabriella goes back to her room to play with dolls and talk to her cousins on the phone. I take Kaden in the living room so he can crawl around on the carpet and sing his famous da, da, da song. Over and over, he sings it like music to my ears, not. Rafael comes in the front door two hours later and gives me the biggest hug and longest kiss.

Rafael and Nakeya began talking. You missed me? I always miss you when we go out of town. Gabriella comes down the steps as soon as she hears her dad's voice.

Gabby yells, Daddy, Daddy you're home? You bring me back something"? Gabby really not all the time you get stuff, but then he went into his bag and pulled out something? It's a snow globe and some jewelry. She loves jewelry. She has at least fifteen bracelets, six watches, thirty rings of all different colors and designs. More to add to her collection. Yeah, I guess the Princess can never have too much jewelry.

Rafael gives Kaden a gift. Here this is for Kaden and gives him some type of soft plush toy and he loves it. He puts him back on the floor and he begins biting on it because he is teething. All he has been doing is drooling lately.

Nakeya and Rafael are still talking. There is something in here for you too? Oh, really and he pulls out this shirt with matching pajamas? I love characters in my pajamas, that's the child in me still. I began to kiss him and thank him for my gift.

Nakeya and Rafael get interrupted by the phone. Allison is in labor? She's really in labor this time. We get the kids together and head to the hospital to meet the newest member of the family.

Rafael and Nakeya are still talking as they are driving to the hospital. Rafael says hey what did you want to talk about? It sounded important. We can talk later. I want to get there to see our new nephew born and give Allison some support? She probably is cussing out people including your brother? We go to the front desk to see where she is and we see the rest of the family in the waiting room. Then we hear Allison tell someone to shut up. "Knock me out and the nurse pointed in the room. I peeked my head at the door.

Allison tells Nakeya to come in here? You sure? Yeah, I want some drugs? I don't want to go all natural, knock me out? Oh no another contraction? How many centimeters? They told her six in a half? What you say? Knock me out I can't do this?

Allison asks Enrique can you get me some ice chips?

Enrique go right now replies Allison? Sure, babe and hurries out.

Nakeya tells Allison to calm down and breathe? Do your breathing techniques from class? In with your nose out with your mouth? See its working. When you get a contraction, it will help with the pain. Enrique comes back inside the room. Allison seems a lot calmer.

Nakeya replied to Enrique, "your welcome? Then they asked to check her after an hour, and they went outside and started talking?

Allison, Enrique and Dr. Onye are talking. Dr Onye says I need to take a sonogram. Something wrong with the baby? No, the baby is fine. I'm looking for something else? She begins to start the sonogram having the monitor facing just her. Oh my God? Dr Onye, what's wrong? We have to take it? I have some good news and I have some great news? Which one do you want? Either one? well you're going to get some medication to take the edge off of your contractions. And you are having a boy? Yeah, you told us that already? Surprise that there is another baby a girl? What, they begin to give her some medicine to relax and get ready to do a C-section because the baby girl is breech? And she can't come out that way.

Enrique tries to get Allison to focus because she's freaking out? Allison, I'm right here, we got this baby? Enrique two babies? Allison, I love you and I'm going to love our babies?

All the family is waiting. We are in the waiting room, and they look at us as they roll her for her C-section. Two for the price of one not funny Juan? No worries, you have family to help you? You're in good hands. Enrique begins to tear up and Rafael rubs his back.

Rafael goes to Enrique to calm him down. You two will be fine. We are familia [family] and we always help familia [family]. Mom and Dad begin to pray and smile at the two babies. My dream was correct she says. I also saw two more babies? Juan and Lydia? Not us I'm done don't drink the water? Then they turn to us? What maybe one day not now? A few minutes later, Enrique comes out and says Ignacio Giovonni Romas is six pounds and, five ounces, sixteen inches long and Ignacia Giavanni Romas is six pounds, 0 ounces and fifteen inches long.

Nakeya and Lydia love the names and then we turn our attention to the nurses rolling the babies to the nursery to do some tests on them both. Then we see Allison, she looks so pale. She has lost a lot of blood, and the family has given her some blood. She will need to get some rest. Dr. Onye will check on her in the morning. Allison dozes off and the family go look at the babies in the nursery. They are so Adorable. I never knew I could love anything or anyone more than I love mami and papi [mommy and daddy] but I do?

Enrique says to the babies Mi tu amor mi Nina y Nino mucho, es mi familia mi Corazón [i love my girl and boy a lot. my family, my heart] . We are family and we will take care of each other because we are family no matter what. He looked at me and it hit me like it was directed towards me, maybe the guilt eating me up? We stayed there and then we all were talking in the waiting room getting stuff for Ignacia a car seat, some clothes, pampers and some other odds and ends to help Allison.

The whole family went shopping and went to their place and started getting the nursery ready for two babies instead of one. So Enrique comes home and gets a bag for Allison and the babies, he comes in and we cook dinner and we do stuff together and he just gets so happy and he said I have the best family.

Enrique, Thanks us all for helping. No problem our pleasure we replied while still working.

Enrique tells us about Allison's recovery. Allison is still a bit out of it. Dr Onye tells the nurse to give her more fluids and some iron to boost her strength and asks her if she felt up to breastfeeding the babies? Yeah, sure let me try little man first? He feeds well then, she begins to feed tiny mami [mommy] at first she doesn't latch.

Nakeya told Allison to reposition herself and then she started eating. Allison and the babies will be going home in a few days, they want to make sure Allison is fine and make sure she is producing enough milk for the babies and, before long Allison was producing more milk the more, she fed them the more milk produced.

Allison talks to Nakeya asking some questions. She looked down at her breast. Is it normal that my breasts hurt so bad? Yeah, and they are huge? Welcome to motherhood 101. Ignacia started crying and she looked I'm leaking. Use your pads, it will protect your shirts.

Nakeya and Allison are still talking about how they're gonna help. I just checked on the babies and they are looking great. Now can I check on you? So, we step out and wait for the results. We start making a schedule about which days' work better for who? So, we can give them a hand with the babies? Either to cook or help with the babies, run errands until Allison is better?

Maria helps Allison get dressed and the boys help Enrique get the car seats ready in the truck. I'm glad he got an SUV.

Nakeya starts to get Ignacio dressed and ready to go home.

Lydia gets Ignacia dressed and ready to go home as well.

Rosetta packs the stuff up and makes sure they don't leave anything in the room.

Then Enrique started pushing the babies out and then the nurse started pushing Allison out in the wheelchair to the car.

All the family in separate cars start heading to Allison and Enrique's place and all the family start to unload and get them settled. We take the babies and place them in their beds that are matching but in different colors. Then Allison lays down and we bring her dinner so she can get her energy to feed the babies at night. Before we leave all the whole family make sure all are, ok? And if they need anything to just call? You have extra food in the fridge, clothes are done, the nursery is stocked, more is in the closets, the kids' clothes are also in the closet and in their dresser drawers, your breast pump is by the bed. Formula is in the kitchen cabinet over the microwave, and all our numbers by phone. Rosetta tells Allison and Enrique word of advice try sleeping when they are sleeping so you two finish eating and try to take a nap.

Nakeya and Rafael get home. Nakeya carries Kaden to his room and Rafael carries Gabriella to her room. She's gotten big and both the kids have fallen asleep in the car.

Nakeya and Rafael begin to talk again as they get ready for bed. So are you going to talk about what's bothering you? I turned around you could always tell whenever I was troubled. Yeah, so talk to me?

You can ask me anything? He touched my face with his hands, anything? So, I start off don't get mad then start telling him everything in the emails that Mona sent before she died? Then I told him about the stuff Alec told me but left out his name. He got up out of bed and looked at me and said, are you sure you want to open that box? I need to know if I'm your wife? I feel like I don't even know you? So he starts telling me and then he stops, goes downstairs, and I follow him. He pulls out all these papers and pictures of him and Glen and then he says, are you ready to hear about how Mona fits into this? Part of me wants to say, no but I say sure to continue. Then he started then he said remember when you had your affair and I left? Tears began to fall. I don't think I want to hear anymore. I left and met up with Mona at her house and we slept together?. He tries to hold me. Don't touch me right now? Keya, I'm so sorry. Wow you slept with her, and you never said anything? I should have told you when we started a clean slate? I know I shouldn't have gotten mad because I had the affair first and he forgave me despite what happened? I think you need to sleep on the couch or in the guest room tonight? Nakeya my love. Please Rafael, please do this for me? I walk up the steps to our room. He comes up the steps and he hear me crying. I know it broke his heart. He always told me he hates to hear me cry. The next morning Maria is there, and she says the kids are with Rosetta. Maria tells Nakeya she talked to her brother, and he told her what happened, that he was so upset. Where did he go? He went to the office to look for you?

Nakeya tells Rafael to please call her phone or the house and that she still loves him. We can work on this. He didn't answer his phone straight to voicemail.

Nakeya asks Maria why he go to the office? If he calls tell him to stay, there. The door is open when she gets to the office then.

Nakeya yells for Rafael baby you here, Rafael? Oh my God, No?

159

Nakeya calls 911. Can you please send the police to 9213 Carmel Drive. There has been some sort of an assault? There is a lot of blood on my office floor. Please, I need help, can't find my husband? Rafael baby, are you hurt, are you here Nakeya still yells until the police show?

Nakeya is talking to the cops. My husband's truck is parked outside. I called for him, but he didn't answer. I saw all the blood on my office carpet. Is there anyone I can call? Vivian, my secretary? Ms. Vivian, this is the police. Can you please come to the office if there has been an accident? Nakeya tells Juan to grab Jose something has happened to Rafael. Please come to the office. Don't tell your parents just yet? Let's see what happens first. We tell Enrique he wants to be here. We told him to be there for Allison and would keep him posted.

Nakeya starts talking to herself crying. I don't want my last memory of him to be of us arguing. I still loved him. I need to ask you some questions. I walked to the front to tell him what happened. Juan and Jose are talking, and they say they are going to go see if anyone saw anything? Nakeya gave the cops the security tapes from earlier? They started looking at the footage and they saw something. They wanted to protect my feelings, but I could hear the commotion. And then I could hear the glass breaking. All I did was cry. Jose tells Maria what happened over the phone. Vivian tells me to go home to wait and pray? I tear up. When I got home Maria hugged me and just told me to pray? All I could do was think about us arguing and telling him to sleep on the couch? What if that was our last night? What if that was our last time?

Nakeya and Rosetta are talking. All of a sudden start feeling so nauseous? I will make you some tea. Did you eat this morning? No well you need to eat and then try to relax? What do I tell Gabriella?

Rosetta tells Nakeya she told Gabby, her that Daddy is on another business trip she got mad? What if he is? We will cross that bridge *when we get to it now eat?*

Nakeya calls her parents and tells them what happened? Her mom wanted to know if Nakeya wanted them there? She replied no for now but she or someone would keep them updated?

Nakeya dozes off and dreams about last week when we were on a romantic getaway. Woke up and remembered today he is missing after our argument last night? Tears fall on the pillow as I drift off to sleep again?

Maria is talking to Lydia, and I just lay there thinking about Rafael?

Lydia asks Nakeya how she feels now from earlier?

Nakeya replies that she is still tired and my stomach is in knots. Well you have been through a lot and busy working on the case.

Nakeya checks her phone for new messages. No new messages.

Nakeya tries to text Rafael again but notices he hasn't checked the last ones?

Nakeya prays to herself, please God make sure he is safe? Rafael, wherever you are, hope you are safe and that you come back home to us? Meanwhile in a warehouse across town. Rafael is tied up and bleeding from his head. The guys that got him hit him with something and dragged him out. Police are reviewing the tape back at the station and keep on trying to see a face or something to give them a clue? They see it was two people but then when they slow it down. They get a partial license plate. On the far side of town, the guys who kidnapped my husband beat him up and he is starting to lose consciousness.

Nakeya jumps up off the couch. He's in pain holding her stomach like she senses his pain? Where is my Rafael, he's hurting? I feel it he needs our help?

Maria comes over and hugs me trying to calm me down. That night

Lydia and Juan come over with the girls so that I wouldn't be alone with the kids.

Nakeya replies I appreciate your company and tries to rest on the bed but can't sleep?

Nakeya goes downstairs to make herself some tea goes to grab a mug out of the cabinet and throws it down?

Juan comes running down the steps to see what's wrong and he sees Nakeya crying uncontrollably.

Juan just hugs trying to calm her down. It's going to be ok. We will find Rafael.

Nakeya tells Juan that she wants him back? She needs him back and loves him. Lydia comes down the steps and she gets on the other side and they both hug Nakeya.

Nakeya does nothing but cry and pray for the safe return of Rafael?

Maria, Vivian, Liz and Karim have been holding down the office. Nakeya's mind is on trying to find her husband and not on Glen's case?

Nakeya decides to share the new information even about my husband and Mona with Maria and Karim? And let me tell you it didn't go well.

Maria and Karim both looked at me like I had three heads?

Nakeya replied I had my reasons for holding out this information? I didn't tell them about Alec? I can't deal with that confrontation right now?

Nakeya decided to touch base with the cops. Good morning. Can I talk to the officer that is working on the Romas case? You can tell him that it's his wife? They have a few leads that you are following and will keep me posted. I appreciate it, I will try to stay strong.

Nakeya pleads to God while praying Rafael baby please send us a sign of where you might be, or who might have you? The kids are taken care of.

Nakeya goes to the kitchen and makes a cup of coffee, but I take it to her office and try to catch up on some work? I start reading over the notes they have taken and then receive a new message?

Nakeya texted Alec and she tried to talk to him he doesn't care? You need to meet me in a couple of days in Nakeya? Alec replies, Nakeya I'm ready to collect? Alec, I can't deal with you right now? It's nothing personal but I will get in touch when I know he's home safe?

Alec texted Nakeya again. Bing, new message? Maybe you're not hearing me? I said I'm ready to collect and won't take No for an answer? Let me text him? Hello Alec, something happened it's bad?

Nakeya says my husband is missing and my mind is on him right now. But when I know he is safe? I will let you collect you got my word? No new message? Now I'm afraid he can't be trusted, and now I'm more nervous? Nakeya gets bad anxiety and worries? What if he comes for my family? A week passed and then some news?

Nakeya gets a call from the police saying they found Rafael? Alive but he has some bruises?

Nakeya starts screaming and they come running in the living room. They start looking sad? They found Rafael and he's alive? They are taking him to the hospital? They all start heading to the hospital and find out what is going on with Rafael?

Nakeya sat in the car for a minute to tell her parents the good news. And a new message appeared? Alec texted Nakeya it read "You need to get ready for my collection"? "I will give you a few days"? Nakeya just stared at the message and teared up?

Nakeya deleted don't care about Alec? My baby is found alive? I walked in and saw them rolling him in on the stretcher. I leaned over and kissed him on the lips.

Nakeya whispered to Rafael in his ear "the past is in the past and I love you and I'm here? Rafael tells Nakeya he's sorry for hurting her as he holds her hands?

Nakeya kissed him longer and told him to get checked out?

NaKeya says I'm not going anywhere Rafael, she's waiting?

Dr. Yin tells the family they will keep him for a few days? He is dehydrated and has a mild concussion.

Nakeya replied I'm going to stay with you, and we can talk if you want? I can just hold you? Baby, whatever you want to do? We can do? I want you to stay and hold me and see if we can start making u?That night I climbed into the hospital bed and kissed my husband. And then we made love in the hospital bed. I didn't worry about Alec and him wanting to collect to keep our secret meeting? All I was doing that night was show how happy I was to see my husband back? My only focus was satisfying my husband and getting back to our happy family?

Nakeya scratched his scalp as he slept. Thinking about how she was going to keep the meeting with Alec a secret? And not to lose her family if he finds out what will happen? The next morning,

Nakeya left to get Rafael some clothes and things he asked for? And grab a shower change my clothes, grab an overnight bag as well.

The cops came to ask him some questions? Rafael replied to cops he didn't know who hit him or why they took him?

Nakeya walks from her car in the parking garage to the hospital. Alec comes up behind me and he puts his hands inside her. I told you Nakeya? I own you and can do whatever I want when I want? I will try to move at first. I can't and then he hears a noise? And he leaves.

I pulled myself together and walked back into the hospital acting like nothing happened?

Rafael got all the stuff you asked for, your laptop, your sleepers, and your chargers?

Rafael, did I forget anything? He gets up and he says yeah this?He holds me tight in his arms and kisses me. Not in front of your parents Rafael and laughs.

Gabby says Mommy misses you. Daddy, how are you doing when you come home?

Rafael replies getting better and can't wait to get home to see my babies? Gabriella has been asking about you and we told her that you got hurt on the job, but you are still Super Dad to her? Tomorrow you can go home if you get a good bill of health, and your pressure is down?

Nakeya asked him some questions later that night? Do you know the guys who did that to you? No and I don't know why they just beat me up and kept me tied up. I thought I lost you? You didn't lose me don't think like that? I'm here and I love my family. We start packing up all his stuff and checking out all the discharge papers. But before we finally got home. He decides to go get some lunch with the family?

So we met up with family and we decided to eat lunch together.

Nakeya asks Rafael if he is feeling ok or does he need to rest?

Rafael replies all I need is to be close to my wife, my kids and my family because I didn't think I would see any of you again?

Rafael teary eyed talking to Nakeya. Do you know how many times I prayed to God to help me get away and come back to you and the kids? You and our kids were my main concern and the more I asked the more pain I went through but, as long as I got home, I endured.

Tears filled her eyes. I love you Rafael more than you know? He grabbed my hand and said no one will ever break this family, Ever?

Rafael and Nakeya are still talking while visiting family. We talk about spending time together. Sounds like what the Dr ordered considering what we just went though, we all need some much-needed rest and relaxation time away from work and, get some de-stressing about work blues.

Nakeya starts thinking about Alec's threats and gets a worried look? How are we getting along and don't want it to end? All that goes on in my mind. When is my happy world going to get blown apart? And it will be unhappy and dysfunctional? My face starts to show what is on my mind as he squeezes my hand.

Rafael tells Na'keya no stressing I'm home now and we can start looking forward to our future. I gave a half grin.

Nakeya is still worrying about Alec? No one at the table knows what I still have to face? Better yet who I had to face? Satan himself? He didn't have to worry about anything because he could be in plain sight and no one even know? That's the scary part. He could be right there looking at the family? Mostly me and plotting his next move? Maybe I should tell Rafael and see what he suggests? Who am I kidding? They would see each other, and they would try to kill each other? Maybe if I do this Alec will leave me alone for good? All this worrying is making me feel sick to my stomach?

Rafael tells Nakeya maybe you need to go home and rest? You're working too hard you need to ease up.

Nakeya replies to maybe you're right? I need to work less hours? Who am I kidding? I would just work at home in my office.

Rafael tells Nakeya we can leave in a little bit and the family is enjoying your presence. I'm enjoying family time.

Rafael tells Nakeya we can cuddle when we get home, and I will take a few days off and concentrate on your recovery. I'm stronger than I ever was. This whole situation made me dig deeper into myself and I was determined to survive? I came home to my favorite girls and my little man?

Rafael thank you that kiss made me feel better already.

Rafael replies in her ear ? Maybe we can pick up where we left off in the hospital? You are so nasty Rafael you need to rest. I will afterwards. We were having so much fun.

Rafael tells the family it's getting late, and we have to get Gabriella to bed.

Jose says yeah, we have to get the boys ready for school tomorrow too.

Lydia replied we have to get the girls to bed for school as well.

Nakeya and Rafael started their way home. Nakeya remembered that she needed to get a few things for the house, some milk, cereal, eggs, creamer and some type of meat to cook for dinner? I would go grocery shopping in the morning. Quick stop at the pharmacy to pick- up your medicine they left a message saying it was ready for pick-up an hour or so ago. Traffic is very busy tonight.

Nakeya and Rafael are talking in the car. Maybe we should have left earlier, now it's past her bedtime. NaKeya it's not that late it's only six thirty? Rafael noticed in the mirror Gabriella fell asleep in the back and so did Kaden.

Rafael asked Nakeya what does this traffic remind you of?

The time when we were in Argentina? We were trying to go on a quick trip, and we got caught in traffic because of a bull or something was running on the road.

Nakeya says when you were missing did some thinking.

Rafael replies Naeya we don't have to talk about that.

Nakeya replies back yeah, we do. When I thought I lost you. I didn't want our last memory that I had of us to be negative and that I didn't want to say I forgive you and I will forever love you, Rafael.

Finally, the cars are moving and now we can head home. It seemed like it took forever but I'm glad we had a chance to talk Nakeya? I needed to get that off my chest. I'm glad you got it off your chest. Nakeya starts to panic when she notices a familiar car? But why was it here? And what was on their mind?

Rafael asks Nakeya who was in the driveway. I don't recognize that car, do you?

Nakeya replies maybe they are just turning around?

Nakeya knows and starts to shake and thinks to herself? It's one of Alec's men. This can't be happening?

ABOUT THE AUTHOR

Lakesha Dorsey Maldonado was born and raised in Howard County. She is a proud mother of three grown kids: Amanda, Daisha, and Izaiah. And a grandmother of two grandkids, Javier and Luna. She is a woman of many hats from working as a housekeeper to working in retail. She loves to read books and watching Ghost Adventures, anything paranormal. Her favorites are romance, adventure, and action/horror. Her favorite writers are Sharai Robbin, Terry Mcmillan, Toni Morrison, and Maya Angelo, just to name a few.

It's not just one type of book style that interests her. She wants to write a book that anyone can relate to, not just women but men as well. Her hobbies include playing games on Facebook, writing poems, reading books, and spending time with her family. She hopes to become one of those famous authors. She hopes that the authors she most admires read her books and feel the same way about her. She hopes to one day move to Vegas, her favorite place to visit, and continue to pursue her passion for writing. This is just the beginning?

Printed in the USA
CPSIA information can be obtained
at www.ICGtesting.com
LVHW011928140924
790867LV00020B/386

9 781964 234243